About the Dybbuks, Jewish Historical Fiction From Pittsburgh's Hill District

About the Dybbuks, Jewish Historical Fiction From Pittsburgh's Hill District

© 2016 Sue Lindenberg McClelland
Cover photo by Ellen Weiser
Kimberly Burnham @ Creating Calm Network Publishing Group

ISBN: 978-1-937207-21-2

Jewish Historical Fiction / Religious Studies / International Studies / Family Relationships / Immigration

$12.95 US

About the Dybbuks, Jewish Historical Fiction From Pittsburgh's Hill District

Sue Lindenberg McClelland

Dedication

To my father, Sydney (Lindy) Lindenberg.

Acknowledgements

I extend my thanks to the people of the former Irene Kaufmann Settlement (IKS) who were willing to share their stories and recollections of the past.

About the Author

Sue Lindenberg McClelland is a retired Marriage and Family Therapist with an additional master's degree in Fine Arts and Fiction.

She grew up in Pittsburgh's Hill District, where her father, Sidney Joseph Lindenberg (Lindy) had spent his childhood as a first generation son of parents who had immigrated from Riga, Latvia in the early 1900's.

As part of her master's degree program at Eastern Washington University, she wrote "*About the Dybbuks*" which is a series of interconnected short stories "my father never told."

It is based on snippets of the stories her father did tell and interviews of people who also grew up in the Pittsburgh's Hill District.

Table of Contents

Prologue

Beneath the world there lies a world exactly like our own with fields and forests, oceans and deserts, cities and towns. Its ceiling is the bottom of our earth. Day and night the light is dim, restless thunder groans and yet is never spent. The wind is trapped in deserts, fields, and towns.

The spirits of the dead dwell there. Their transparent bodies slip easily through the membrane that separates their world from ours. Hidden among us in holes and crevices, they peer out and gossip among themselves about our daily lives, except for those whose flames are snuffed before their time is through. Like gutted candle wicks in hardening wax, they lie entrapped in the tangles of unfinished stories and unsung songs.

Slowly they wake and stretch their faces toward those of us who breathe fresh air to melt the wax that seals their lips and tell their stories to the end.

~Adapted from S. Ansky," The Dybbuk"

I am Sue Jean, daughter of Sidney Joseph, granddaughter of Sarah Judith. The letters S and J, curving initials we three share, unravel the edge of the curtain which separates my world from theirs. Spirits wake and stretch their slender arms, grasp my fingers and whisper to me in airy voices: Ezra, Hyman, Sarah, Golda, Nathan, Lindy, and Alfie. My heart is full of them. I yearn to lay them down to rest.

I grew up standing on the fault between two worlds, a swirl with slender filaments of memory as delicate as spider webs. In the fall of my seventh year, before I started second grade, our family moved from a shaded residential neighborhood in Chicago to Pittsburgh's Hill District, a place of steep cobbled streets lined with tenements and storefronts. Here, my father had been delivered by a local midwife on October 20th, 1908, the third son of Sarah Avner and Herman Lindenberg, who had come to America from Riga, Latvia. Yiddish was the language spoken at home by his parents, aunts, uncles, and most of the other Eastern European Jews in their generation.

Masses of Jewish, Irish, and Italian immigrants occupied the Hill District when my father was a boy—peddlers and stogie makers, butchers and housemaids. Once they discovered that the gold that paved those cobbled streets could only be bought by hard work and ingenuity, people broke their backs to make it happen.

By the time we moved there in 1947, the Hill had become a different place. Gone was the cacophony of Yiddish, Irish, and Italian accents. Ours were the only white faces in a sea of black. We lived there six years. Yet somehow in that short time, the spirits from my father's world rose up and filled a room inside my soul.

A yellowed clipping dated November 1st, 1947, tells of our arrival in the city: Pittsburgh Press Salutes Sidney J. Lindenberg's Return to Hill District as Irene Kaufmann Settlement Director. And underneath in smaller print—IKS Kid Returns Home.

The article refers to my father as Sidney J. Lindenberg, nicknamed 'Lindy,' and quotes him: "I grew up just a few blocks from here. The Irene Kaufmann Settlement was my second home. It was right here I decided to become a social worker and dedicate my life to helping other people move upward from the ghetto."

The Hill District certainly needed help. The burned out buildings stood abandoned. Their walls were thick with graffiti and windows were plywood or cardboard covered scars. Debris littered the streets and alleys; broken bottles, batteries, torn paper cups, even an occasional abandoned car, its windows broken and insides gashed. On my way to second grade at Miller School, I stepped over the splayed out legs of men passed out against tavern walls, their dark-skinned faces bruised and swollen, shirt or jacket fronts stiff with dried vomit.

The clipping I hold in my hand sixty-six years later crumbles at the edges. I am far older than my father in this picture.

The settlement years were good for Dad. He truly had faith in the American dream that children of immigrants and the underprivileged would leave the ghetto and move up in the world. He believed this with all his heart. Many of them did. His career is woven into the history of the Settlement Movement, a reformist social movement, beginning in the 1880s and peaking around the 1920s in England and the US. The goal was to get the rich and poor in society to live more closely together in an interdependent community.

My father's boyhood is embroidered on the tapestries shared by the thousands of children, who played stickball, tag, and run-sheep-run on those steep crowded streets. He didn't like to reminisce about his youth. He only mentioned it as a unique snippet of his professional resume. Instead he filed that childhood ghetto underneath his waking memory, and, like a forgotten shadow, it always trailed behind him.

My brother and I grew up in the building Dad had called his second home. We ran his cobbled streets and alleys. Our footfalls kicked up buried tracings of our father's boyhood shoes. And though we pestered him, he found excuses not to take us to the house on Cliff Street, where he was born and that had housed Lindy's, the family grocery store.

That first year on winter evenings when dad had retired to his armchair, I would crawl into his lap and ask him questions. He would never answer. Instead, he would distract me with offers to brush my hair, or raise the ever-present *Pittsburgh Press* and read to me from current events.

Almost everyone near and dear to my father had died early and, devoted as I was, I merely felt protective as his only Jewish daughter. More likely though, moving to the neighborhood where he had spent his boyhood caused my feet to slip through a fault in the earth to that ghetto of old, where gloomy *dybbuks* waited to come forth.

At night, the streets below my bedroom window were alive with quarreling voices. Even an occasional gunshot pierced my sleep and became tangled in dreams of a dark-haired woman called Sarah. She wore a high-necked-old-fashioned dress of blue plaid gingham, covered with a large white butcher's apron, its strings wrapped around her slim waist and tied in front. Her face was partly shadowed by long black curls, too exuberant to stay confined in the hairpins she used to anchor the bun at the nape of her neck. I never saw her eyes, until at last she turned and I was looking out of them.

In my childhood synagogue, only men prayed openly, deep voices beginning the familiar words of the ancient *Kaddish*—a prayer for the dead. *Yarmulke* covered heads, dark red, brown, bald, black and curly, yellow *tallit* fringes moving gently to and fro, a waving wheat field of golden light, chanting in rhythmic cadence: *"Yitkadal, v'ytkadash sh'mei raba."*

It is not possible to translate the prayer into English. Jewish law prescribes the recitation of *Kaddish* by at least ten men, each morning at sunrise for one day short of a year following the death of a loved one. No one prayed *Kaddish* for my father. The few men in his family who lived according to Jewish law sunk beneath the veil before him. Each time I walk into a synagogue, I am haunted by certain faces—the fine cheekbones, slanted foreheads and narrow skulls of the family that call out to me. And so I write, black letters of fire burned into white paper. The match I strike burns through the night on the outlines of their stories. I light the candles of their lives and walk with them between two worlds.

Streetcar

Pittsburgh is carved out of the base of the Allegheny Mountains, at the juncture where the Allegheny and Monongahela Rivers merge to form the great Ohio. In the summer of 1907, Center Avenue, in the city's Hill District, was a five block strip of small businesses whose wares overflowed into a street already lined with peddlers and pushcarts. Their owners hawked a variety of merchandise from fresh pretzels and apples to plumbing supplies and women's hats. Mothers with babies in their arms and toddlers clinging to their skirts bargained for fresh produce. Knots of old men chattered and argued in heavy accents while children played at marbles, or tag, or stood watching at the edges of the crowd. The groan of wheels or the clatter of hooves alerted the throng to divide and make room for the trolley, the ice wagon, or the fire wagon drawn by two stallions with red ribbons twisted in their tails who stepped into their own harnesses whenever the fire bell clanged.

The Pittsburgh Hill District is aptly named. Some of the hills are so steep that the row houses look as if they might topple, or their many occupants spill out the open windows onto the cobblestones. Cliff Street, where my father grew up, angled up so sharply that a special trolley had been put in so people could get back and forth from town. The streetcar groaned its way upward, inch by inch, with passengers clutching the metal poles as if somehow they could prevent the car shattering its moorings and careening backwards to the bottom. The downward pitch was accompanied by whispered prayers for the lasting strength of the brakeman.

One hot, sooty day, several years before my father was born, Nathan, his eldest brother, sat shooting marbles on the front stoop of Lindy's Grocery and Deli. Nate was seven then, and he'd just completed second grade at Miller Elementary. A layer of smoke hung over the neighborhood from the steel mills across the river. Nathan was bored. He yawned, but didn't want to take a little nap like Mamma had suggested. The flat was a regular *schvitzbath*.

A chair propped open Lindy's door. Nate glanced inside. The store was quiet. Most of the customers had come by in the morning. His mother dozed beside the buggy where his brother, Alfie, napped. Big flies buzzed over the baby, silenced only when they hit the long strip of flypaper that dangled from the ceiling.

Alfie stirred and began to whimper for the third time in half an hour. Nate's Mamma stuck a worried face through the screen door. "Naydie, be a *mench* and take the baby for a little walk. He's so fussy. Walking will make maybe a little breeze for him."

Before Nate had time to answer, she'd maneuvered the buggy through the door and parked it in front of him. Then she tucked three pennies in his trousers pocket. "Buy for yourself a little treat, Son. A shaved ice, maybe."

Waves of heat rose around his ankles from the blistering street. Vinegar steam drifted from the pushcarts on Center Avenue. Nate licked salty droplets from his upper lip, thinking the moisture might quench his thirst. A mother walked by. She is large and panting with a child hanging on to her. Pulling a kerchief from her hair, she wiped her forehead and her children's runny noses.

The baby was gurgling and playing with his chubby toes. "Hi Alf."

He gave Nate a one-toothed smile.

"Nice ride, Huh?" Nate was thinking what kind of shaved ice to buy. Maybe strawberry. He imagined the red sweetness melting on his tongue. He'd stick his finger in the paper cone and give a taste to Alfie. Nate slipped a hand in his pocket and counted the pennies. One, two, three hard-edged discs. All there. If he had an extra, he could put it on the trolley tracks like the older boys did. He'd keep the flattened disk in his pocket and rub it for good luck.

All at once, the buggy wheels stuck in a rut, then jarred up on the other side. Startled, Nate relaxed his grip. As the handle slipped and the buggy lurched ahead, Nate stretched his arms but the handle bobbed in the hazy sunlight just out of reach. Just then, a thick piece of soot pricked Nathan's eyes. He tripped and grazed a knee, stumbled up, panting.

At the top of Cliff Street, metal wheels beat a tat-to-tat against the tracks as the trolley began its hourly plunge. The brakes screeched. Passengers stood open-mouthed, peering from the stairs and windows. Nathan stood with empty hands and watched the red and yellow streetcar ram Alfie's buggy off the tracks. His brother flew into the air, with wide eyes and arms flung out, then bounced across the cobblestones and lay still.

The trolley ground to a halt, but the roaring in Nathan's ears kept on. People crowded around, their bodies melted into his like candle wax. Alfie lay there on the street, the pale blue blanket Mamma had fixed up for his buggy ride flung casually across his tummy. A bruise spread, like a puddle of wine, across the baby's forehead. His heart must still be beating, for blood to pump into a bruise like that. Alfie's eyes were staring out, as blue and still as glass. Nate knew they would blink in a second. Then, all the people would go home.

Two men were bending over the baby, tapping sausage fingers on his chest and head. Nathan wanted them to leave his brother alone. Behind them on the street stood the conductor's black shoes and wrinkled pants.

Glancing up Cliff Street, Nate caught sight of Mamma rushing downward in the silver air with her apron flying. Black hair fell in curtains from her bun. She shoved her way up through the crowd, knelt on fingers splayed across the cobblestones and laid her ear on Alfie's heart. Nate watched her reach into her apron pocket for her glasses and holds them near the baby's mouth. He held his breath, praying for a wisp of steam to cloud the glass. The faces of the crowd stared up from the shiny circles, each one a shrunken image of the faces looking down.

Then, as if she'd merely stooped to change his diaper, Sarah picked the baby up, spread his blanket on the ground, and bundled him in a neat blue triangle. When she'd raised him to her shoulder, she rose, swaying on unsteady feet.

The crowd stirred, and a path opened. Aunt Golda walked up to Sarah and wrapped an arm around her shoulders. Staring straight ahead with tears sliding down the creases in her cheeks, Golda guided Mamma through the press of curious faces.

A hand settled on top of Nathan's head. He turned and saw his father's face, his lips the color of ashes. They barely moved to form three words, "Oh, my G-d."

Nathan took his father's hand and felt its dampness on his palm. Then they walked beside Aunt Golda, Mamma, and the silent baby, past the ribbon of storefronts, past pushcarts, past faces that looked like frozen cries, toward the temple, Beth Harushan Shul.

Maybe Rabbi Goldstein could think of a way to start up Alfie's breathing. He hadn't stopped that long ago. Besides, he looked as good as new except for the bruise. The air inside the synagogue was cool, and Nathan shivered. His Mamma's face was soft with tears that made a wet spot on her apron bib. The Rabbi hardly looked at Alf. That was a bad sign.

The grown-ups talked a long time. Then Rabbi Goldstone knelt and took Nate's fingers in his big warm hands. The roaring stopped in Nathan's ears and the room was still. "Nathan Aaron," said the Rabbi in a voice as gentle as the white hair that tumbled on his forehead. An ache started to grow in Nathan's chest. "A terrible thing has happened today. A brother is special. He cannot be replaced."

Nate looked at Alfie, small and still in Mamma's arms. He remembered the one-toothed grin, the tinkling laugh, the round little body that struggled to sit without tipping over. The ache exploded in his throat and he was choking on his tears.

"Sometimes the Holy One perplexes me," said the rabbi, as he pressed seven-year-old, Nate's hand and blotted his cheeks with a clean white handkerchief. "It would seem you are young to bear such a trial. Even though it will be years until your *Bar Mitzvah*, Nathan Aaron, I would like you to come to *shul* each morning and chant a *Kaddish* for Alfred with your father. A year of mourning will perhaps allow the Holy One to grant you peace."

***

Nate helped Mamma and Aunt Golda turn every mirror in the house to the wall and cover up the windows with rags.

"Why?" he asked.

Golda told him that back in Russia the Old Ones gossiped about tormented souls that lingered. *dybbuks*, they were called. If a newly dead spirit saw its face reflected in a mirror or window, it might get stuck behind in the world of the living. "*Dybbuks*," Golda added, "are probably a bunch of superstitious malarkey."

***

Alfie was buried in a steamy sunrise. The collar of Nathan's Sabbath shirt pinched the back of his neck and Mamma's keening hurt his ears. He watched the mourner's throw dirt over a small wooden box. Shovelfuls struck the lid and muffled as the hole filled up.

He imagined Alfie waking up inside that box, reaching up to touch the lid. His brother didn't like the dark too well. He'd whimper a few times and then warm up to a bellow when he realized he was stuck. Nate clenched his fists to keep from grabbing a shovel and digging Alfie right back up. Instead, he lowered his head, like Mamma and Pappa, and rocked to the rhythm of the burial chanting and the tap-tapping of the shovel backs as they firmed the growing mound of dirt.

Sitting *shiva*, Pappa told Nate, was a little like having company for a whole week. You had to be polite. Women from the *shul* brought food. A circle of men stood in the living room four times a day and chanted *Kaddish*, their bodies leaning to and fro in cadence with their voices.

Inside the flat, Nate thought he heard a baby's laughter echo from corners and behind doors, begging Nate to play peek-a-boo. Even though Aunt Golda didn't believe in *dybbuks*, Nate knew that Alfie was one. His mother and father never really said the accident was his fault, but Nate felt as if he'd committed murder.

Again and again, he went over the details. He saw himself daydreaming about the shaved ice, fingering the pennies in his pocket. He watched the buggy jar, the handle slipping from his hands, his legs pushing the heavy air. How stupid he was! Worse than stupid, evil!

On the fourth evening of *shiva*, Nate walked into the living room. His father's body was slumped in an armchair. "Pappa?" he swallowed.

Nathan barely raised his head. "Please Pappa. It's my fault." Then he was choking. Tears were dripping. "The buggy slipped. See? I was checking in my pocket. See?" He showed his father how he'd checked. "I couldn't catch the buggy because I was thinking about the shaved ice." His father sat completely still. Speak, Nate commanded silently and clenched his fists. To hear his father's voice would be a relief no matter what he said. Nathan wished he could curl up in Pappa's lap with his big arms around him.

"What's done is done, Son." A deep red crack cut his lower lip in half. His mouth wrinkled as he said, "Accidents happen. The Holy One gives. He takes away. God knows why."

"Pappa, listen," Nate pressed on, "The Lord didn't take Alfie away. I killed him! I let the buggy get away." He was yelling now. "Pappa please, I made a murder!"

"So what, Nathan Aaron. *Nu*? So my son is dead. Your brother is dead. All your chattering and blaming yourself, it don't bring him back. Shut your mouth already. It don't help. My heart is broken. Reassurance, God help me, I can't make for you."

Nathan's brain was about to burst. He couldn't stop himself. He had to know. "Pappa, what happens to you when you die? You know, where do you go after?"

"When you die, you're dead. That's all. The grave diggers bury you in the dirt. Quit talking about it, Nathan."

"Pappa?" "Stop it with the questions, Son." Hymie stood up. "Who do you think I am, the prophet?" He headed for the kitchen.

Nathan stood there, licking tears and listening to a voice behind him repeat the somber warning that he'd lost his one best friend.

The week of mourning came and went. Nate suffered endless chunks of honey cake stuffed into his mouth by the fingers of sad-eyed, motherly ladies. "Here try some of this honey cake I brought for your Mamma. It's still warm from the oven." Nate thought he might hate honey cake for the rest of his life.

On the sixth day he heard children's voices shouting outside in the street. A fireman cranked the cap from a rusty hydrant. A torrent of water whooshed into the street. Children shrieked with glee, splashing in the puddle. He could almost feel the water streaming through his hair. How he longed to jump into his shorts, dash out of that mournful flat, and run with his best friend, Joe.

On the seventh day, they cleaned the house, shined the mirrors and turned them back to reflect their own sad faces. Early in the morning for a year, Hymie got Nate out of bed and took him by the hand to Beth Harushan where they chanted *Kaddish* for Alfie. Soon Nathan knew the prayer by heart: "*Yitkadal, v'ytkadash sh'mei raba. Y'hei sh'mei raba m'vahakh l'alam, ul alme almaya. Omen.*"

Kaddish was all that was left of Alfie now. That and the nightmares. Every night Nate listened to the crunch of the streetcar hitting the buggy. He watched his arms stretching, his feet pounding, as if he could run fast enough to follow Alfie right into the world beyond our world.

Making A Comeback

Sarah kept telling herself losing a child was not that uncommon, as though somehow that would make her baby's passing acceptable. Only two doors away, twin girls had weakened and died of tuberculosis that past winter. Every August, the dreaded polio seeped through the ghetto on a steamy haze and struck the homes of its chosen with the certainty of a biblical plague. A few weeks before Alfie's misfortune, a child had been trampled under the hooves of the fire wagon horses while her mother haggled with a peddler over the price of tomatoes.

She floated through the days, her ears turned inward to the whimpers of a baby she could never soothe. Her dress hung loosely from sharp shoulder blades, and her hair slipped from its pins in unbrushed chunks. She took to wearing house slippers, brown suede with yellowed fur, which whispered on the hardwood floors. Fridays she prepared the Sabbath meal in numb compliance with ritual, though she no longer believed in God. Spider webs of fog clung to her eyelids. She performed her daily chores with sluggish hands.

Her vision dwindled to the tiny circle of the immediate. Each day, she put off returning to the store, saying to herself, "Tomorrow is soon enough."

One November afternoon, she sat swaying back and forth in the warm spot by the kitchen stove. The wooden rockers squeaked on the hardwood floor. As her hands plucked at the dry cloth of her black skirt, her fingers felt the softness of a cotton diaper. Her mind came loose and drifted. The baby lay below her on the double bed, squirming, and kicking as she tried to fasten the second pin in his clean diaper. With deft hands, she pulled a shift over his head, then swooped him up and buried her nose in the soft folds of his neck. His laughter fluttered on her cheek.

All at once, a hand was tapping her shoulder. A whiny voice grated its way into her daydream. "Mamma, Pappa wants to know, where is the lye? The ice box leaked. It stinks awful."

She opened her eyes. Nathan stood beside her. She stared at him. No plump or winsome baby this. Seven years old, skinny, and rough-skinned. The scrawny forearms, chapped hands with bitten fingernails, the pinched and mournful little face with a thumb-print of purple below each eye, scratched across her reverie like sandpaper. "*Gotenu!*" she muttered to herself. "For this I came to America—this clumsy son who let my baby's buggy slip. Better I should have stayed in Riga and been raped and murdered by a Cossack!"

Hymie hollered up the stairs. "The lye is hiding perhaps?"

"In a minute," she shouted back. "Patience, Husband. Enough!"

Sarah raised her weak body and shuffled to the window. Framed against the pewter sky, her reflection was the color of oatmeal. A jagged row of icicles rained sooty droplets on the street below.

She patted her disheveled hair and smoothed the wrinkles in her skirt. Her slippers thudded down the stairs. When she flung open the door to Lindy's, the door chime clattered to the floor. The can of lye was sitting in plain sight on a shelf at the back of the tiny storeroom.

"Nate," she hollered in a sour voice and he came running. "There," she jabbed a finger at the can. "Two parts water, one part lye, Nathan Aaron. And, don't splash, you'll blind yourself."

Then, since she'd already made the trip downstairs, Sarah wandered over to the counter and took her place behind the cash register. Her hands knew how to do their work: to sort eggs by the dozen into cardboard cartons, to grasp the metal scoop and dip pale yellow butter from its barrel in perfect half-pound slabs.

Her hands knew to grip the stub of yellow pencil and tally sums on a white curl of paper.

Her's friends welcomed her back. They held her icy hands and tried to massage a little warmth back into her fingers. The face she turned toward them was a face they didn't know, cut by two creases from eye to chin as though her tears had worn their own crevices. Without curiosity or recognition, she swept up coins from friends and strangers alike, as though she were her own shadow.

"*Dybbuk*," they whispered and slipped away, quiet so as not to rouse the restless spirit. Soon the door chime went silent. Hymie stood behind the counter with his arm around his wife, and watched their customers pass by on their way down the block to Finkelstein's emporium.

One day he took her cheeks between his palms. "My wife."

She looked.

"I have heard them gossiping. Some say Alfred's *dybbuk* has spoken to them, beside the shelves or in the back. They are afraid the evil eye will catch them if they come into the store."

"*Kvetching yentas!*" Sarah spun on her heel. "They would ruin a business with their chatter?" She raised a hand when Hymie moved to follow. "Stay here!

Husband. In back, there is waiting for me plenty of work. First, that stinking ice box."

So she rolled up her sleeves and attacked the ice box in a whirling cloud of lye. She scrubbed the wooden pickle barrels with a stiff-bristled brush, the stinging in her fingers a reminder that life blood still flowed beneath the skin. Taking a screwdriver, she pried the tops from dusty boxes and stocked the empty shelves. As she moved about, her body thawed.

One spring day, she heard voices up in front. Her husband, wearing a clean white butchers' apron, stood on the street in front of the store. "*Shalom*, Mrs. Schwartz." His voice rang out with just a little too much *shmaltz*. "Welcome! Come in. Try some of the smoked whitefish. It's delicious today. I've just had a small sample myself." Old Mrs. Schwartz sniffed and nibbled at the tidbit like a dog who wasn't sure if the hand that held it was friend or foe.

"Wonderful whitefish, Hyman," she said, taking a large bite and wiping her mouth on his proffered handkerchief.

"Ah! Mr. Rubenstein. You have been well, I trust. I worried. Lately you have been making yourself scarce. How about a bagel, just out of the oven. And fresh cream cheese?"

The door chime tinkled once, twice. Sarah took a breath, exhaled, and felt the lonely store begin to stir awake. Fingers of glowing light moved down her chest. And in the shadows out of sight her lips curved upward, ever so slightly.

***

Nathan turned eight, then nine. Sarah remembered nothing of those birthdays. His ninth, June 7th, 1910, dawned bright. A thunder shower during the night had cleansed the world of soot.

Sunlight dappled Sarah's bare arms as she lifted buckets of boiling water off the new gas stove and poured them into the enamel tub. Her cheeks were flushed and the strands of hair that escaped from a makeshift dishtowel bandanna curled damply on her neck. Her forearms tightened as she rubbed each item up and down over the grooved washboard.

A loosely tied white apron clung to the growing curve of her belly, the first visible sign of my father's presence in the world. Standing, she wiped her hands on the apron, then toted her wash basket over to the window and began pinning pieces to a clothesline that stretched along a pulley to the building across the alley. Through the zigzagged rows of dripping wash, she spotted Nathan as he rounded the corner of the building on his way home from his morning Hebrew lesson. He barely missed a peddler with a giant sheaf of brooms.

"Nathan!" she called, "Take your time. Do you want to spend your birthday picking up brooms?"

"No, Mamma." Sunshine poured onto the tipped up face. So obedient this son of hers. So grave, almost like a man.

"Perhaps you might find time in half an hour to accompany your Mamma to the ice cream shoppe for a birthday sundae?"

"Oh, yes," he breathed, and smiled.

So, she thought, seriousness is a condition that may be remedied by ice cream. Could the last two birthdays have passed without even a smile from her? She fretted over Nathan Aaron. Did he still think about the accident, and the dark time afterwards, when Hymie couldn't bear to look at him, and she herself wished he'd been killed instead of her baby? Nate had been too small to push a buggy. That much she'd admitted to herself, but not to him.

The heavy fog that numbed her brain and made each step like walking through molasses, had thinned and lifted. Poor Nate! She hadn't been much of a Mamma. She thought about her own mother's death, the loneliness of losing her, and wondered if Nate felt as bad as she had. Quick tears sprung into her eyes. Well, maybe she could make it up to him now.

"Nathan," she called. "Ten minutes! Wash your hands and eat a piece of bread. Ice cream before lunch will sour your stomach." Sarah unwrapped the towel-bandana, brushed her hair, and pinned it up. On top, she set a straw hat with an artificial rose stuck in a crimson grosgrain band.

Next to Nathan, wearing the hat she knew set off her dark hair and made her cheeks glow, Sarah felt like skipping. Instead she took his arm and did a little two step,

"We will do a promenade."

Nathan jerked away. "Mamma!"

"What," she assumed an expression of dismay. "You are too big, maybe, to dance on the street with your Mamma?"

She and Nathan were the first customers in Anna's Sweet Shoppe. They chose a round marble table and two white chairs with twisted metal backs. Reflected in the mirror behind the counter, Anna Feldman stood, in a pink and white ruffled apron, washing sundae glasses. She dried each one on a yellow terry towel and set it on the mirrored shelf behind her.

Sarah reached across the table, shook out Nathan's napkin and tucked it in his shirt.

"Mamma," Nathan pulled it out, "I'm nine years old."

"So," she said, "Nine years is old enough for you to wash ice cream out of a clean shirt?" She flinched, knowing her mock-playfulness was off, yet not knowing how to be natural.

Anna Feldman wiped her hands, picked up a pencil and a small green pad and walked around the counter to their table.

"A Happy Birthday, Nathan Aaron Lindenberg. And good morning, Sarah." She stood by Nate. "Have you decided?"

For endless seconds, he looked down at his bitten nails.

"Speak up!" said Sarah."Mrs. Feldman does not have all day to wait for you to order." There it was again, that edge. She hoped she'd be more patient with the new baby.

Anna glanced at Sarah and swept an arm toward the empty tables. "Time I have. Excuse me, Sarah Lindenberg. A birthday decision is important!" She turned her back toward Sarah, and leaned toward Nate.

A bright pink flush was creeping out of his collar.

"How about three scoops to begin with. Chocolate? Vanilla? Strawberry?"

Nate nodded.

"Which?"

"All of them."

Anna was writing on her pad. "And hot fudge?" she asked.

"That sounds good too," smiled Nathan.

"Nuts? Cherries?"

"Yes!" he nodded vigorously. "Yes. And a little whipped cream and sprinkles and butterscotch and strawberries?" He paused, then glanced at Anna with a little grin.

"Maybe, could I have a small sample of everything?"

"Certainly! A birthday sundae with everything. Coming right up." She put the tail on the 'g' with a flourish.

Sarah sipped her coffee between bites of ladyfinger and vanilla ice cream with butterscotch. Across from her, Nathan dug out spoonfuls of his monstrous sundae and shoved them in his mouth. She struggled to keep herself from taking her napkin and wiping his face. He was finally smiling a bit.

Why couldn't she be playful and make him smile like Anna? Why was she so awkward? She couldn't seem to quite make it up to him for the hatred she'd felt when he killed—when he'd let Alfie's buggy slip. She felt the familiar metallic edge between them. A dead baby and two lost years took some getting over. Why, when she wanted to be kind, was she so often irritable with him?

Nathan ran his tongue over his lips.

Sarah tried smiling. "You're doing such a good job of cleaning that glass, Anna won't even have to wash it."

Nate raised his lashes and looked shyly up at her. "Yes, Mamma. I've licked it clean as a cat."

Settling more easily in her chair, Sarah looked across at him. "Son, have I ever told you about the first time I tasted ice cream? When Golda and Grandpa and I got off the boat at Ellis Island?"

"Yes, Mamma, lots of times!" Nate's chair scraped against the floor. "Um, Mamma, I gotta meet Dave and Ralph at the Irene Kaufmann Center for practice. You can tell me again tonight maybe."

Hesitantly, he reached across the table and patted her hand. "Mamma? Thank you." Grabbing his baseball glove from under the table, he darted for the door.

Rosary

For most of Nathan's seventh year, he and Pappa had gotten up at daybreak and walked to Beth Harushan Shul to say *Kaddish* for Alfred: *"Yitkadal, v'ytkadash sh'mei raba."*

Nate's body and his child's voice were hidden in the chanting of the men. During the prayers, he pictured Alfie's soul, lacy as a curtain, drifting toward the world beyond.

"Today we say the last *Kaddish*," Hymie had announced one Tuesday on the way to *Shul*. Nate ran a little to keep up. He'd grown to love the early morning street. As the milk truck rolled by, glass bottles jiggled in their metal crates. Harry the ice man pitched sideways under the blue-white block he carried to a tenement door. Ahead of them on Center Avenue, peddlers set out their wares. A swarthy man pried the lid from a wooden barrel of kosher pickles, and Nate breathed salt and vinegar. He imagined his teeth popping through the skin of a dill pickle—the squirt of juice, the tingle in his ears.

"Quit daydreaming!" Hymie pulled his sleeve. "About *Kaddish*. We say it for one year. We will not be saying it tomorrow."

Nate wished he felt so certain. "Pappa, could we perhaps say for Alf a few extra *Kaddishes*. Just to be sure he got, you know, got there."

"Whaddaya mean, Nathan Aaron. The Law is from the Holy One. We obey, that's all. No questions."

"Yes Pappa," Nate replied. But something peculiar hovered out of reach.

***

Three years had passed since that last *Kaddish*. More than ever, Nate was certain his father had been wrong. All was not well with Alfie in the other world.

Every night, the terrible message came through his bedroom window on a tunnel of light as smoggy as the day the streetcar killed his brother. Every night, Nathan stood with empty hands and watched the buggy careen down Cliff Street. He saw himself chasing behind, gulping chunks of air that stung his chest. Falling, stumbling up, he limped on with bloody knees. Every night, he heard the screech of brakes, the too soft thud. He stretched his arms, far but never far enough to grab the shiny handle. And Alfie, a triangle bundled in powder blue, flew up in the air with startled arms and soft cheeks and gleaming curls and saucer eyes that never left Nate's face. The nightmare shifted then. The bundle plummeted, hung a few seconds over the streetcar tracks, then arched skyward. And Alfie, still wrapped in his blanket, drifted into the yellowish haze till all that was left was his broken sobbing. "Naydee. Come and get me. Come Get Alfie. Get the baby. Naaydeee."

"Grab a hold of something, Alfie boy." Nate shouted at the sky. "Hold on. I'm coming. Wait for me."

Nathan usually woke then, standing by his bedroom window, yelling Alfie's name into the night.

***

"Pappa, what good was praying *Kaddish* for Alfie?"

Nate raised the troublesome question at breakfast one morning.

"Why would you even ask? The Law is the Law, Nathan."

Nathan laid his fork down and tried to get his father to look at him. "Alfred ain't resting so good, Pappa. Maybe even he's a *dybbuk*. All night I hear him calling, 'Naydee, come and get me. '"

His father's lips stretched in a tight smile. "*Boychik*, you should perhaps go into theater. We have no little *dybbuks* in this flat. See?" He lifted the edge of the table cloth and peered underneath.

Nate didn't even bother looking.

"Soon your Mamma will be having for us a real brother or sister. If you wanna worry, Nate, worry about how to put bread in that baby's mouth. Now there's a worry!"

Nate felt like he was drowning. Why wouldn't Pappa just admit it? He tried again, his voice a whisper softened by a thousand sleepless nights. "Pappa, listen please! Maybe just this one time, *Kaddish* didn't work. Maybe we gotta pray some more. Maybe... "

"The Law is the Law. Twice already I have explained: one year minus a day and not one day more. Do you want to tempt the evil eye?"

"Tempt it...it's already here," mumbled Nate.

"Dammit to Hell," yelled Hymie and grabbed him by the wrist. Fingernails bit into the soft skin.

Nathan rubbed the nail marks with his fingertip.

"You're a mess, Nathan," Pappa's nasal voice droned on. "Start sleeping at night! Have your mother fix you a cup of hot milk."

Nate felt as if he were shrinking. Silky threads twirled through the air and wrapped him in a tight cocoon. His Pappa's words tapped on outside, but he no longer heard them.

The milk was terrible. It had a skin on top that gagged him. And nothing stopped the nightmare. At first, he prayed the dream would fade. After awhile, he just gave up and buried his face in the pillow so Pappa wouldn't wake, hear his screams, and know that he was still having a problem.

***

In the daytime, Nathan's life returned to normal. After school, he played stickball with Ginzy Ginzberg, Dave Levy, and Peewee Schwartz at the comer of Cliff and Center.

The street was jammed with children playing jacks and hopscotch, tossing rubber balls, and shouting to each other.

In the midst of it, Nate and his friends staked out their turf for stickball. Rubbing dirt between their palms, they gripped a sawed-off broomstick. Over and over, they smacked a chunk of wood above the crowd and pulled it from the air with up stretched hands. Women, balancing baskets of eggs and fruit, trailing little children in their skirts, hollered at the boys to quit before they broke a window or gave someone a concussion.

David's mother helped him wrap a ball of yarn with sticky black tape and after a few clumsy tries the boys learned to play with a ball.

Early that summer, a stranger appeared in the neighborhood. He had brown curly hair, straight teeth, broad shoulders, and muscled forearms. Sometimes he would stand on the corner and watch the boys play stickball. They wondered aloud among themselves, "Who was the man and how did he get such impressive muscles?"

"I think he's about twenty-three and lifts weights," suggested Ginzy, whose older brother was twenty three and lifted weights.

"Mind if I pitch a couple?" the man with muscles asked one day.

"Pitch?"

"Yeah."

"Sure. Okay." The boys were perplexed. No adult they knew had ever had the time or inclination to play stickball with a bunch of kids.

Nate tossed the ball.

After a few pitches, the guy was giving pointers. "Feet here," he adjusted Peewee's stance. "OK, now. Choke up a little on the stick."

Peewee hesitated, cleared his throat and blew a spit wad at the stick. "Good job, Pee," someone muttered. The others swallowed snorts and brays.

Ginzy had to walk away a minute to get hold of himself. He held the stick between his thumb and forefinger and shook it. The wad of spit stretched to a thread and dropped. The man wiped his hands on his pants. "U-uh, Kiddo. Choke up on your grip. Like this."

Afterwards the boys stood wiping sweaty foreheads on their sleeves and shirttails.

"You guys ever play baseball?" asked the curly-haired man.

"Never."

"Nope."

"We're poor."

"Who's got money for equipment?"

"We saw a Pirate's game last year," said Dave, his eyes bright with remembering. "At Forbes Field ... the IKS chartered a streetcar."

On that special Sunday, they'd sunburned their noses in the stands, grabbed popcorn by the fistful from a butter-spotted paper bag, jumped up and down on the rickety bleachers, and yelled till they were hoarse.

"I have a couple bats and balls," the man broke in. "My name is Ziggy Kahn. I'm the new Athletic Director at the IKS."

"Dave,"

"Ginz,"

"Peewee,"

"Nate."

He shook each boy's hand in turn.

"I'd like to start a baseball team, maybe even start a league. I've talked to several other guys."

"Wh-what's it gonna cost us?" Nate stammered, afraid the price would prevent it.

"Free memberships for ballplayers to start with, at least this summer. About a penny a day for milk. If that's too much, talk to me privately."

The next morning Ziggy met his ball team in the newly opened IKS Milk Stop. The place looked like a classy restaurant. Plants hung from the ceiling. "Drink milk to grow," a large crayoned mural above the counter advertized. Below the letters was a drawing of a sad, skinny boy going into the Milk Stop and a happy and fat coming out.

The boys lined up for milk, one cent a glass, and graham crackers, four squares to a napkin, then squeezed their chairs around two tables pushed together.

Finally, Ziggy wiped his mouth, wadded his napkin and leaned on his arms. His chest and shoulders looked enormous compared with the twelve scrawny would-be-ball players he had recruited. Nate sucked in his breath, pushed out his chest, and squared his shoulders.

"Welcome!" Ziggy said, "I'm glad to see you drinking milk. Next few years, you'll grow a lot. You'll need at least three cups a day."

"Today is a special day," the coach continued, propping up a small plywood framed blackboard. He drew a baseball diamond in squeaky yellow chalk and put an X on each position in the field. The twelve boys voted to call their team the Maccabees—second century Jewish warriors who led a successful revolt against the Greeks.

They were a ragtag group. Shoes were the biggest problem. Most of them wore hand-me-downs, black leather high tops with long frayed laces—too large, too small, even two different shoes. Still, they maneuvered in the painful footwear, or played barefoot, cleaning cuts and gashes with witch hazel until their feet grew hard as leather soles.

After several weeks of practice, Ziggy gathered them at home plate. "Boys, I have exciting news. We're going to play a few games with another team."

"Who are they?"

"Are they any good?"

"Oh heck! I bet they're better!"

"I spoke to Father Pat at Saint Teresa's." Ziggy went on. "He has a new team too—the Crusaders. He says they're eager to play some real games."

"Pardon me, Mr. Kahn," Dave interrupted. "You're saying we're supposed to play guys that jump us on the street, force us to pull our pants down and beat us up because we're Jewish? My Pappa would not like for me to play them."

"Mr. Kahn, they hate us."

"We'd have to defend ourselves...."

"I peeked in Saint Teresa's once." Ralphie Shapiro, the youngest Maccabee was bouncing on his toes. His eyes were huge. "There was two big idols in there—a lady in a robe and a man without no clothes at all, except this little *shmate* tied right here." He drew a finger from hip to hip below his belly button.

Eleven pairs of eyes followed the finger.

"Oh Ziggy," the voices rose to a crescendo. "Can't you find a Jewish team for us to play?"

"Just a minute." Ziggy's voice was curt. "You know as well as I do, you're the only Jewish team. Maybe someday there'll be more. That's really not the point though. America is a free country. Baseball is a game and not a war."

Looking back years later, when all of them were men, the boys would realize that was the only time Ziggy Kahn was wrong. To begin with, the Crusaders were taller by at least a head. No one even cared to guess their weight—it was too depressing. The first three games were shut outs. After the team handshake, the Crusaders headed for the locker room, shouting taunts behind them at the losers.

Losing every single game was terrible for Maccabee morale. "We gotta develop strategy," Ziggy encouraged. He outlined plays in squeaky yellow chalk and walked the team through every one until it was nearly flawless.

They won the fourth game eight to six. In the fifth and last game, the score was tied in the bottom of the ninth, and the Maccabees were up at bat. With two men on base and one out to go, Nathan Lindenberg smacked the ball over the right fielder's head.

Three pairs of legs circled the bases in perfect beat with one another. Three wiry bodies crossed home plate. Nate slid in a split second before the ball slapped the catcher's mitt. Maccabee discipline collapsed completely. The players ran around yelling, smacking their hands together, and pounding each other on the back. The Crusaders ignored the handshake altogether and walked off the field in a grumbling block. Suddenly, the tallest Crusader on the team turned and cupped his hands around his mouth, "We won't touch your filthy paws," he hooted. "They're covered with the blood of Jesus Christ!"

"Murderers," the others heckled, picking up his drift.

Nathan's teammates had lifted him high in the air on a chair made of their arms and were parading him around the field.

"Murderer," the word echoed in his ears. It hit his brain and spun his head around. How did they know? Shame swirled like nausea inside Nate. They couldn't know, he told himself. The Crusaders, with their snarling mouths, were calling every Jew a murderer. Trembling with rage, Nate jumped down from his victory seat and tore across the playground. His right fist hit the big guy's teeth. Blood spattered on his hand and wrist. As he drew back to strike again, the anger vanished.

The big Crusader wiped his lips and spit a mouthful of blood onto the dirt. Then, without a sound, he picked Nate up by the seat of his pants, carried him across the playground and flung him into the fence.

Nate slid down the bumpy chain links and sat on the dirt, shaking his head from side to side. He took his nail and began to pick the gravel from his knees. His 'victim' shrugged and turned to go.

"Hold it, Tim." Father Pat's arm came out and blocked the big Crusader's exit. Nathan looked up into a circle of startled faces.

"This is a disgrace." Father Pat cast a sour look over the gathered players.

"Crusaders, I'm not proud of you, especially of you Tim McEnery." His grabbed McEnery by the neck of his T-shirt. "Nor of you, Nate Lindenberg, if you don't mind my saying so. Christ says turn the other cheek. Maybe you guys don't know what that means."

He nodded toward the Maccabees. "But every one of you has heard of sportsmanship ... "

Two teams nodded, staring at the ground. Ziggy Kahn walked over and put out his hand to help Nathan up. "Stand right here, Nathan. Move in closer, every one of you, Maccabees and Crusaders. Now, look each other in the eye. What do you see?"

"Boys."

"People, same as me."

"Ballplayers."

"Right! Jewish ballplayers and Gentile ballplayers. Who knows what it's called when different religions talk and act as if they hate each other?"

"It's mean."

"It's called prejudice! We saw movie about it in school."

"Exactly! It came into the world long before you were born. So you didn't start it. It causes problems though. Little problems, like a fight on a ball field. Big problems, like wars and pogroms. In Russia, Nate might have been shot for raising a hand to a Christian."

Ziggy walked around the inside of the circle. "Two boys had a fight on a ball field and we are standing here talking about it. So we've already made some progress."

Twelve sets of Jewish eyes focused on Ziggy—the broad forehead, brown hair that curled below a baseball cap turned backward, generous lips, the only Jew they knew who spoke without an accent. To them he was a prince somehow, all they ever hoped to be.

"I'd like to have you shake each others' hands now. And as you shake, introduce yourselves. Like this." He walked over to Father Pat and stuck out his right hand.

"Hello, I'm Ziggy Kahn."

"I'm Father Pat O'Leary."

***

Nate felt a little unsteady on his way home and stopped to sit a minute on the curb. The black, white, and gray pebbles around his shoes swirled. He closed his eyes and put his head between his knees. In a few seconds, he felt a large warm hand on his shoulder. Turning, he stared up into the wide face and broken mouth of Tim McEnery. He stumbled to his feet.

"Are you OK?" McEnery asked.

"Yeah. Stopped to rest a minute. I was just leaving." His temples were pounding.

Tim reached out to steady him.

"Easy, now. I didn't mean to scare you."

Two soft hairs were growing from McEnery's chin. His lower lip was bruised and swollen. Nate felt better just looking at it. "Gee, Tim. You're lip don't look too good," he said.

Tim poked it gently with his finger. "Aaah! Ain't nothing a little ice won't fix. I been hurt lots worse. Got six brothers. I'm the baby. They beat me up for fun!"

Some baby! Nate looked up at Tim. He had brown eyes, with straight brows almost the color of his freckles, and a voice as deep as Pappa's. Nate took a few shaky steps, and Tim fell in beside him.

"Boy, was I mad," Nate confessed. "I was burning up! I would have hit you no matter how big you were."

"I came looking for you. I'm sorry, Nate. You're coach really made me think. He's quite a guy."

"You really have six brothers, Tim?"

"Yeah, not one sister or even a girl cousin in the lot. Just boys, two of 'em already men."

With all those brothers, Nate wondered to himself, could a person maybe afford to lose one and not feel so bad?

"I have a brother. He's a baby. Cries all night long. A person can't get any sleep. I can hardly stand him. A long time ago, I had another brother. I liked him.... He died though."

"Oh yeah?" Tim turned, "How old was he?"

"Six months, I think. His name was Alfie...Alfred Moishe Lindenberg. When I was six, he died in an accident." Nate wondered why he was talking so much.

Tim walked alongside, his long legs pacing Nathan's shorter steps. It was a real *schvitzbath*, a steam bath of a day. Mamma had me take him out in his buggy. She gave me money for an ice ball. It slipped— not the shaved ice, the buggy did. The handle, the metal ... you know. It was slick with sweat." Nathan's throat ached. "You see, I really am a murderer. That's why I had to hit you, Tim."

"I don't get it, Nathan."

"Well, listen! The buggy headed down the hill. I ran twice as hard as that home run today. Hands missed the handle by a Goddamn inch. Alf was sleeping. He flew up. Light, kind of. He opened his eyes. The blanket hardly even mussed. Even after he was dead, he kept staring at me." Nate rubbed a grimy wrist over his eyes. "I have the worst nightmares!"

"Ain't surprising," Tim commented. "Did you go to confession?"

"Confession?"

"You know, for when you sin. Your church don't have confession?"

Nate shook his head. He didn't even know what sin meant.

"You go into this little booth inside the church and tell the priest the things you did wrong. It's private. Except when he sneaks a look at you through this little hole in the wall. Anyway, you say what your sins are, and he tells you how many Hail Marys to say. So Jesus will forgive you. Then it's over. That's all." Tim snapped his fingers.

"Just like that!"

"Hail Marys?" Nate echoed.

"Yeah. Like a song with two verses. Wanna hear it?"

"Sure."

"Hail Mary, full of grace," Tim began in sing-song, "The Lord is with Thee. Blessed art Thou amongst woman and blessed is the fruit of Thy womb, Jesus. Holy Mary, Mother of God, pray for us sinners, now and in the hour of our death. Amen."

"That's nice, Tim. What does thigh-womb mean though?"

"I dunno. Must be Latin. It ain't the words anyhow. You kind of get the beat of it." Tim kicked a stone.

"We said Kaddish for a year. That's a prayer too. To help Alfie's soul to rest. Some rest he got. He's a *dybbuk!*"

"A what?"

"A *dybbuk*—a homeless soul, a ghost, a demon ghost. All night he screams at me to bring him back. I think God maybe sent Sidney to take his place. I loved Alfie. Sidney, I don't even like."

Soon they were approaching Cliff Street. "Hey, I turn here, Tim."

Tim faced him. "All right, Nathan. Maybe I'll see you. I hope we get to play again sometime."

Nate shuffled his feet. "Tim?"

"Yeah?"

"Thanks." He spun around and ran the whole way home.

***

Baby Sidney's nightly wailing threaded through the barrier of Nathan's sleep. The nightmare began to change. Alfie's cries grew angry as he rose into the air, his face blue-red, contorted, his tiny mouth twisted in rage: "Hurry Nathan. Faster. I'm suffocating. G-i-v-e m-e y-o-u-r b-r-e-a-t-h."

In the darkened room, Nate screamed too. He no longer bothered to put his face into the pillow, but added his cries to Sidney's in a mounting nightly dirge. "*Shanda!* Shame," accused the voices in his dream. Dreamtime fingers pointed at him.

Even when he would grow to be a man, a father with a wife and children, he'd still be a killer. He wondered if he could catch pneumonia like Fanny Appelbaum upstairs. She went easy, his Mamma had said. Maybe he'd go easy too. He thought about stabbing himself with the silver blade his grandfather, the *Shohet*, kept honed to a killing edge. And he thought about confession.

The idea slipped into the nights and soothed him. He imagined telling some priest that he'd killed his brother—that he owed it to Alfie, some way he didn't understand, to hate Sidney forever. He whispered what he could remember of the Hail Mary Tim had said for him. And his lips felt soft. After practice, Nate sometimes took the long way home, past Saint Teresa's.

As he was going by the arched doorway one day, he caught sight of a bearded figure in a dingy overcoat shambling toward him on the sidewalk. The man wore the greenish-black felt hat of a *Chassid* ... Rabbi Schwartz, his Hebrew tutor! Nate could practically smell the sour breath in the shut-up room where he went each morning to practice reading *Torah* for his *Bar Mitzvah*. Without thinking, he ducked into the entryway.

The smell of candles drew him toward the sanctuary. Three dark wood tables were covered with them, their flames reflecting blue and orange in shiny pools of wax. He walked to the closest one, behind a back pew. Leaning over, he felt their heat warming his cheeks and forehead. The candles smelled like toasting marshmallows.

Objects took shape in the dimness—rows of hard-backed pews with kneeling boards behind, the rounded back of a woman praying, head resting on her arm. Other people came and went, knelt to pray or contemplate. Some waited next to two varnished wooden booths with child-sized doors.

The air Nate breathed seemed different from any he had ever known. He pictured a boy who looked like him removing the black satin *yarmulke* he had worn to pray since he was small and tucking it into his knickers pocket. Then, in a waking dream he had rehearsed for weeks, Nathan Aaron Lindenberg, son of Hyman Lindenberg and Sarah Cohen, grandson of Moishe Landerman and Ezra Cohen, stepped bareheaded down the center isle of the Cathedral of Saint Teresa of Avila. The fantasy faded away.

Light filtered through colored windows that looked like puzzles made of broken glass—shepherds with staves, a man and a woman with a baby on her knees, the same man staggering, supported by his friends. He must be the one called Jesus. Nathan followed the strip of maroon carpet. Two large statues filled the front of the cathedral. A woman in a blue robe was standing to his left. In the center, high above the altar, a man was nailed up on a giant cross. My God,

Nate thought—and actually apologized in case God heard him—they really do have idols. He waited for Jehovah to come in and strike him dead. Nothing happened.

The woman's foot rested on a blue globe with a snake wrapped around it. Marble hands were folded over her pale blue robe. Her cheeks were brushed with pink, and a shawl that matched the robe covered her head. Her eyes were blank holes—like Nate's picture of Shloime, the blind beggar.

He walked up three carpeted stairs and stood below the crucifix. Bare feet hung over his head, so lifelike he could see the sinews and a thin wash of blood below the dark holes that nailed them to the cross. The Jesus had shins and calves as perfect as the young men who steamed themselves in the IKS baths on Sabbath eve. A blue cloth, knotted below his navel, wrapped his hips and abdomen. Ruby drops oozed from two puncture wounds on his ashen chest. Rusty-looking nails held his arms and hands outstretched on the wooden cross. Nate stared at his bearded chin and the angles of his cheeks. He felt shy to look at the face of someone in such agony, yet couldn't turn away.

Waiting for the person in front of him to finish with confession, he noticed a space between the wall of the wooden booth and the floor. The priest's foot, in an ordinary man's shoe, was covered partway by the hem of his black robe. Nate opened the tiny door and sat on a narrow bench in the dimness. He took a breath.

"I pushed my brother underneath a streetcar. I didn't mean to. The buggy slipped," he blurted at the wall in front of him. "I already tried *Kaddish*. It's, urr, a Jewish prayer. It didn't work. I'm still a murderer. I have terrible nightmares. I wish I could die."

Nate stared at the filigreed wall. He thought an eye was peering between the carved leaves. Not caring for anything except that the priest behind the wall lift his burden, he shoved his kinky hair behind his ears.

"Now young man, begin again." The voice was gentle, with a heavy accent. "This way. Bless me Father for I have sinned."

The second time went better. Nate told the voice about the streetcar. He told the voice how much he hated Lindy for taking Alfie's place and making Mamma and Pappa forget.

The voice spoke. "May your courage in coming bring you ease, Son. Accidents are not happy. But God is kind. He understands. Your brother's soul is safe in heaven. You may grow to love the baby brother." He paused, thinking. "Twenty-five Hail Marys seems not too excessive. Yours is a special case. Say twenty-five now, son. And go in peace." Slowly, the priest went over every word, as if he thought Nate might not know them.

Sitting in the hard wooden pews, Nate repeated the prayers over and over, counting on his fingers. Aching sobs forced their way up and out his mouth. His body rocked to and fro with the rhythm in his bones, the age old cadence of the Hebrew *Kaddish*. Remembering Alfie, he cried for the baby, the boy, even the man his brother never would be. He imagined telling Alfie not to worry in the other world, that Sidney was a whiner and a *nebbish*. In a million years, he never could take Alfie's place.

After awhile Nathan looked up at the woman in the blue robe. This time, when she looked down, her eyes were alive. She had the kindest face he'd ever seen. He said an extra twenty-five Hail Mary's for good measure.

The Cat

My father, Sidney, was only two weeks old when Hymie carried him in a new leather carriage down the steep tenement stairway to Lindy's. Sarah followed, with her sister Golda holding an elbow to steady her. Halfway down, her knees gave way and she collapsed onto the stair above. "Rest a moment with me, Golda. I'm a little worn out."

"Worn out?" Golda placed dry palms on Sarah's cheeks and peered into her face.

"*Gotenu*, Sister, your color is atrocious. Let me help you back to bed before you work yourself to an early grave for that husband."

Sarah pressed her lips together. Golda was an old maid. What did she know from marriage? Sarah gripped the railing, dragged herself up, and reached a foot down to the stair below.

The scents of pickled herring and salami enfolded Sidney in his buggy. Customers came and went to the tinkle of a door chime. They hung their faces over him and *kvelled* in squeaky voices. "Lindy," someone called him, and the nickname stuck for life. Awake, Lindy lay with his mouth pursed like a wise old man and peered into space as if trying to discern shapes in a mist. At five, when he got his first pair of glasses, his mother would remember the baby squint and imagine he'd been nearsighted from birth.

When he was hungry, Sarah would carry him to an ancient rocker hidden in the shadows of the storeroom. There, she'd gently sway and catnap while he nursed. For weeks, those bits of stolen sleep were all the rest she got, since Lindy split the nights with restless crying. Afterwards, she would remark to Golda that all of her memories of Lindy's first year seemed like dreams, since she had spent the whole time sleepwalking.

Nate avoided the buggy. With its bright chrome frame and handle, it looked stronger than old gray one the streetcar hit. The new buggy was the color of the horse-drawn hearse that came down Center Avenue whenever someone died. To look inside was to picture the face that never would be Alfie. To imagine the handle in his hands was to feel it slip away. Nate knew he'd have to push the baby some day. Yet, he kept hoping the day would never come.

A couple of months later, he streaked past Lindys on the way to sign up for basketball at the IKS.

"Naydee?" Mamma called out the open door in a wheedling voice. "A beautiful October we are having—the afternoons are warm."

"Yes, Mamma."

"The baby is cooped up all day in the dark store. He's getting the color of a pickle. He needs fresh air and sunshine to make him pink again."

Nate felt like a chicken must feel when its neck is about to be blessed with the *shohet's* blade.

"So now, my Son...Beginning with this afternoon, you will come home after *cheder* and take your brother for a buggy ride."

Brother. He flinched. "M-mamma, could I maybe take him tomorrow?"

"Tomorrow it could rain. He's all ready." She glanced into the buggy. "See how he is looking forward? I'll help you push him out the door."

"Mamma? I'm scared."

"Look at me." Sarah pushed his chin up with her index finger. "So then, my son, you are not feeling so brave?"

He nodded, ashamed.

"Five years ago, you were a little boy—now you are a *mench*. Your arms are strong. Here, make a muscle."

Nate bent his arm and squeezed his hand into a fist.

Mamma poked the muscle with hard fingers. "Tough as iron. See Nate? Besides," her voice grew husky, "the Angel of Death will not strike twice in the same place. I have never heard of such a case."

Turning, she opened the screen door. Her black hair was pinned up in a loose bun. A few stray curls lay soft against her neck. To Nathan, she was the kindest, most beautiful mother in the world. For her, he would scrub wooden barrels till his hands were chapped and pricked with splinters. He would drag fifty pound sacks of flour and potatoes from the storeroom. He would even push Lindy in that buggy.

Fists clenched around the shiny handle, Nate glued his eyes to Lindy and started off. One, two ... three steps. As he walked, holding on so tight his wrists ached, a roaring started in his ears. A streetcar! Peering sideways up the hill, Nate caught the gleam of trolley tracks and children playing in the hazy light. When he glanced back in the carriage, the baby lying there was Alfie. He tried to yell, but made no sound. The roaring in his ears was deafening. All at once, the buggy thudded to a stop.

"*Gotenu*, boy," shrilled a voice. "Eyes were made for looking where you're going. Are you blind?"

A woman was rubbing crossly at her bulky plaid hip. "You could cripple a person!"

70

In the midst of the chaos, Lindy opened his eyes, twisted up his face, and howled. When Nate brushed back the baby hair and smoothed the puckered forehead, Lindy closed his eyes again. Blonde lashes lay against his cheeks. Not dark lashes. Nate forced himself to pay attention ... not Alfie.

He decided he'd wander past the IKS playground. His friends were lined up shooting basketballs into two hoops at either end of the dirt court. In white canvas shoes with rubber soles, Ziggy Kahn ran back and forth shouting pointers. Nate wound his fingers through the chain link fence and concentrated on getting Ziggy to look his way.

When the coach caught sight of him, he bounded over to the gate and opened up the padlock with a key from a jangling ring. The gate swung out on rusty hinges.

"Nathan," Ziggy clapped him on the shoulder, "I hope you are turning out for basketball. Your friends are in great need of you." Ziggy helped him push the buggy to the sidelines.

N-no Coach. I have to watch the baby for my mamma. Inside the fence with Ziggy and his friends, it seemed foolish to be scared. There were no streetcars on the playground. And Nate's hands ached to touch the ball.

The coach poked his head under the hood of Lindy's carriage. "Your brother's fast asleep, Nate. Try a shot or two. Go on! I'll keep an eye on him."

Nathan didn't need a second invitation. The basketball slapped against his palms. When he aimed, time stopped. The ball tapped dead center above the hoop, slid through the string basket, and bounced back on the court.

"*Mazeltov!*" yelled Ziggy. "Perfect shot."

The muscles in Nate's thighs tingled, tempting him to play some more. Basketball and baseball too, were effortless. His body knew just what to do. Without thinking—like a bird flying.

"Thanks Coach." He tossed the ball to Ziggy, checked Lindy, and sunk down cross-legged on the gravel beside the buggy.

A large yellow-brown cat with a dirty white bib was loitering on the street outside the playground. Drawn by a faint milky smell, it sprung to the top of the chain link fence, dropped inside, and skulked over to Nathan and the baby. One amber eye was staring straight at Nathan. The other was glued shut by an edge of sticky pus. After sniffing Nathan's shoes and the buggy wheels, the cat tensed as if to spring into the carriage. A majestic orange and gold striped tail jutted to the left of center from a raw looking patch on its hindquarter.

"Hey!" Nate laid a discouraging hand on its matted back. The cat flopped over on its side, purring like a rusty motor. A putrid smell rose from its fur, somewhere between sour milk and rotten gefilte fish.

"*Feh!*" Nate shook his hand, wiped it on his knickers, and turned to watch the action on the court. It was almost like a dance—feet slapping, ball bouncing on the ground, the sharper tap of ball on wooden backboard, a chorus of whoops and groans. Ginzy shot a foul that rolled around the rim for endless seconds before it finally dropped inside the hoop.

"Yeah! All right!" Nate hooted encouragement with the rest.

"Mmmrow!" bawled the cat, springing up on all four legs as if it was cheering. Moments later, when Lindy began to cry, the cat bolted upright again, and split the air with sharp meows.

"Well," said Nathan, "I'll be damned."

Every day the cat would hop the fence and plop down on the gravel beside Nate and the baby carriage. As soon as someone hollered, or Lindy even whimpered, the cat would start its restless howling.

Nate brought a hairbrush and a tiny silver scissors from home. Gently, he snipped at the tangled matted bits and brushed the heavy fur. He put witch hazel on a clean white cloth and dabbed around the edges of the puffy eye. At length it opened showing the gold-flecked amber like the other. The cat grew sleek and handsome, but the rotten odor lingered.

One afternoon, when the ball flew out of bounds toward Nate, he raised his hands and caught it. Then, as if he'd been playing for the whole game, he dribbled out across the court and tossed an easy basket.

Silence. Then his friends turned toward him. "Nate, you just gotta play."

"It ain't natural—you sitting out."

"We need you!"

Every muscle in Nate's body was coiled to spring out on the court. Yet, there was no way he could.

Mac Rabinowitz stepped in front of him. "Nate? Zat yer name? That cat's a born baby sitter. Bet I could train 'im to look out for your brother."

Mac had a heavy Russian-Yiddish accent. Nate had heard about him. His family walked a frozen river to escape from Lithuania. He'd been hanging out in front of *Cheezy's* with the Jewish hoods, when Ziggy met him and brought him to the IKS. Mac had a reputation. He could talk bread out of the baker and extra slices of corned beef out of *Cheezy.* He looked about as rough as the cat.

"How about it Nate, want me to train 'im?" He stood there in a pair of huge black high tops without any socks and short pants that looked hacked off with a knife. His knees were skinned and so filthy Nate

74

thought about cleaning them up a little with the cat's witch hazel. Mac grinned.

"Sure, why not." Nate couldn't help but like him.

"Bring 'at cat some food tomorrow," Mac advised. "An animal don't train good widdout sumpin' to eat."

By the time Nate arrived, Mac had already dragged a chair outside from the Milkstop. Soon the cat strolled across the gravel playground. It rubbed around Nate's ankles, and then sniffed all four chair legs. Mac scooped up the huge body, set it on the wooden seat and pushed the cat's rump down with his hand.

"Cat! You sit there now—Y'hear?"

The cat jumped lightly to the ground.

"Maybe the chair's a little hard." Nate folded Lindy's extra blanket and smoothed it over the seat. "Hungry, pal?" he asked. Pulling a greasy sardine out of his pocket, Nate laid it in the middle of the light blue blanket. The cat hopped up and nipped at it. "Hey! Wait a minute." Mac snatched up the oily thing and bit it in half. "I said sumpin' to eat; that cat don't need a banquet. Ain't no reason to waste a whole sardine..."

He gobbled it hungrily and wiped his mouth on the back of his hand. The cat chewed its half with a burbling purr, then plopped down on the blanket and began to lick its paws.

"Hey, wait a minute. You ain't earned your supper yet." Mac grabbed the animal and sat it up. The cat yawned, curling the tip of its rough pink tongue.

"Watch!" Mac elbowed Nate. "Eeeeooow, get em. C'mon, sink that ball," he yelled. The cat shot up on all fours, with its tail straight in the air, and let out an ear splitting howl.

"See?" laughed Mac, "No problem."

Nate would have dashed right out to join the game. His thoughts turned to his mother, though, with her tired eyes. How she'd trusted him with Lindy, even after the terrible accident he'd had with Alfie's carriage.

For two more days, he sat on the sidelines, flexing his hands and debating with himself. There were no streetcars on the playground, he reasoned, not even out behind on Craig Street. Ziggy and the other boys would help him listen for the baby. And the cat was loud enough to hear in the next block. Most convincing of all, he recalled his mother's blessing. "The Angel of Death does not strike twice in the same place. Son, I have never heard of such a case."

On the third day, Nathan grabbed the cat under the front legs, held it up, and looked it in the eye. "Listen Cat, that's my baby brother." He hung the cat above the buggy. "He's little, like a kitten. See? You gotta watch 'im for me, Cat, as if you was his Pappa. Or I'll wring your neck."

76

He rearranged the cat on the chair. "Holler when my brother fusses." He thumped the cat between the eyes. "Every time, y'hear?" The cat blinked.

"Every day, I'll bring a sardine. Mac won't get it either." Nathan stroked the large head. "Phew! Damned if you don't stink." Shaking his hand, he strode out on the court.

The first few days, Nate practiced basketball with his ears trained on the baby. When the action moved too far, he'd stay behind. And every time the cat meowed, at least three players yelled for Nate.

The afternoons grew shorter, cooler. Sarah tucked a crocheted afghan around Lindy. Snuggled in his warm cocoon, the baby breathed the sparkling air, and his cheeks grew rosy. He began to stay awake awhile and laugh and gurgle at the boys. The cat fluffed out its glossy coat and perched, huge and majestic, on the sitting chair.

Looking back, Nate never could pinpoint the exact moment when he got careless. He remembered changes though—moving further from the buggy when the action traveled down the court, forgetting about Lindy for minutes at a time, trusting the cat to meow loud enough, relying on his friends to hear. When the thought of Lindy crossed his mind, he'd hurry over to check. Once or twice, when Nathan looked across the court, he thought the sitting chair was empty. When he got closer, though, the cat was always there. Perhaps his imagination was playing tricks on him.

One evening, Sarah was folding the afghan, when she thought she detected a faint smell. As the days passed, the scent grew stronger. Finally, she mentioned it to Hymie. "My husband, please to take a sniff of Lindy's blanket. There is something a little peculiar."

Hymie raised the blanket to his nose, inhaled deeply and flung it on the floor. "*Feh*!" he choked, "A terrible smell! Dead fish? A privy maybe...or a lovesick cat. Something is not right."

***

The next day Hymie Lindenberg took a little walk. In the midst of foul shot practice, Ziggy pulled Nathan to the sidelines. "Look," He pointed across the playground. "Is that, perhaps, your Pappa?"

In his black felt hat and unmistakable light hair, a white shirt and a tie pulled open the collar, Nathan's father was striding across the playground. His overcoat flared out like bat wings. His mouth was set in a scowl.

Nathan bolted across the court in time to reach the buggy just ahead of Pappa. Oh God! The sitting-chair was empty, and the cat lay draped across the baby's chest, its claws kneading in and out of the crocheted afghan. "Cat!" Nate gasped.

The cat opened its eyes to slits. Lindy's eyes were closed, one arm flung above his head, tiny fingers curled. Dead, Nate thought, and knew for certain it was so. He put his hands on Lindy's belly.

"*Dumkoph*!" His father smacked his hands, reached for the cat, and flung it out across the playground. The cat let out an angry hiss, the fur along its spine raised in a ridge. Its claws raked Nathan's forearm.

"Cats suck the breath from babies and they die!" yelled Pappa.

The cat hit the gravel and scurried off.

"Pappa...Lindy's dead isn't he?"

His father scooped the baby up. Lindy squirmed, drew up his legs, opened up his tiny mouth and started wailing.

"No, thank God."

By then the boys had stopped practicing and were standing close by. Ziggy walked up and stuck out his hand.

"Welcome Mr. Lindenberg, I am Mr. Ziggy Kahn. My apologies for this unfortunate event."

When Hymie didn't shake the hand, it dropped to Ziggy's side. "Please to know this is not usual, Mr. Lindenberg," he went on. "Nathan, on the contrary, has looked after his brother responsibly—with the help of his friends, of course. And I myself have been keeping an eye on the situation. By the way, Sir, your son is an excellent athlete. You have reason to be proud."

Pappa clutched the baby to him. Lindy was crying steadily by now. Nate reached into the buggy and handed his father a bottle.

"Proud," said Pappa. "Proud? My son the athlete has almost killed another brother. I should be proud?"

"Mac trained the cat to babysit ..." chirped Ralphie Shapiro. Ginzy grabbed him by the hair.

"Jesus Christ!" yelled Hyman Lindenberg.

Ziggy reared back.

"What do you know, young man in your white shoes fit for a *fegeleh*? Do you know my son has murdered one brother already?"

"No Sir." Ziggy shook his head.

"Another buggy, not so long ago, five years maybe, he let get away down Cliff Street hill. A streetcar ... a streetcar hit it." His chest caved in, and his body heaved with dry sobs.

Lindy's tiny hand reached up and touched his father's tears.

"Mr. Lindenberg?" the coach patted his black wool sleeve. "I'm so sorry. I did not know."

Hymie recoiled. "Tell me, young man, have you ever lost a son?" Tears were sliding through his beard now, and dripping on the baby's face. "The evil eye has come into my home. *Kein Ayin Hara,* it will never happen again."

Nate felt as though he was watching from far away. He felt Ziggy touch his shoulder.

"I think it's better if we go now." He gestured to the knot of boys. "Come."

Ziggy walked away with each long arm around three boys. It was right that they should go, Nate thought. His coach would hate him now and that was right too. Being an athlete didn't make up for being a murderer. Pappa tucked Lindy back under the afghan and left pushing the buggy, as though Nate weren't standing there at all.

The sky was gold above the three strands of barbed wire at the top of the fence. Except for Nathan and his thoughts, the playground was deserted. He slid his rear down the fence and sat down on the ground. The metal diamonds pressed into his back through his shirt. Maybe he should run away. He sat there pelting his shoe with rocks, wondering where he could go. Everyone would be better off—better off if he were dead. If he turned around right now, he was sure to see the curtain to the world beyond our world. He thought he heard his brother Alfie calling him.

Earlier that day, he'd been so happy. Where did feelings go like that, when you couldn't feel them anymore? Nate sat there till he was stiff, and his teeth were chattering with the evening chill. Then he sat some more. His throat ached and he needed a drink of water. Above the fence, the sky was nearly black. A string of words tapped drumbeats with the rhythm of his heart, *selfish, evil, murderer* ... Like accusations from the Holy One himself.

Geezer

By the time my father, Lindy was three years old his parents were no longer the greenhorns who'd crossed the ocean in steerage twelve years before. They spoke a little English now, learned bit by bit in night school. Life was work—eighteen hours a day, six days a week—for food on the table, for pens and paper, for Sabbath candles, for Nathan's Hebrew book, for Lindy's shoes and the starched collar Pappa wore to greet his customers. Lindy's Grocery and Deli had gained a cadre of regular customers who paid in cash rather than run up endless tabs, faithfully listed but never fully settled. Early Friday mornings, the women of the Hill District lined up to buy Sarah's Sabbath *challah*. Dozens of the braided loaves, crusty and fragrant from the oven, were snatched up and taken home to grace the Sabbath tables in the tiny flats.

Lindy's grandfather, Ezra Cohen was the *Shohet*. Called the 'Chicken Killer' by the neighborhood children, he slaughtered and blessed the Sabbath chickens. Dressed for the melee in a rusty black *yarmulke* and a dingy prayer shawl with tangled fringes, he'd stalk them on arthritic legs until he'd cornered every bird, wrung its neck, and slit its throat with his silver knife. He hung the chickens upside down along the clothesline. Then, muttering the *kasshruth* prayers, the old man *davened* to and fro. He glanced slyly up at them from time to time, as if calculating the price a particularly fat bird might bring.

Nathan was twelve years old. His voice cracked and his feet and Adams apple had grown huge. He'd begun bumping into furniture and door jambs, as if the flat had suddenly grown smaller. His feet smelled. Hymie slipped his stinking boots out on the stoop to air at night. Each morning before school, Nate read Hebrew with an ancient *Chassid* to prepare him for *Bar Mitzvah*.

Too young to run the ghetto streets, Lindy spent most of his first three years inside the store. His eyes adjusted to the dimness, so much they watered when he walked into the light. He suffered from frequent colds and nightmares, from a big imagination and a big vocabulary. When he'd begun to talk in full sentences at only a year and a half, Sarah, convinced her son was smart enough to be a doctor, began to squirrel away a small nest egg for medical school.

Lindy had stretched into a slender three-year-old with a tangle of burnished caramel curls. Sometimes, Sarah spread the red-gold strands of hair over her fingers until they glowed like honey. Other mothers gazed at him with envy, bemoaning the fact that the Holy One, praised be He, had not seen fit to put such hair upon their daughters' heads.

One day, a customer mistook Lindy for a girl and began to *kvell* to Hymie over his gorgeous curly hair.

"Enough!" The father broke out of his usual preoccupation with things to do and bills to pay. "I will not have these *yentas* making my son into a *fegeleh*." Grabbing a scissors from the cash register drawer, he set Lindy up on the counter, and hacked off the offending curls.

Lindy sobbed through the ordeal.

"So young he is, and already a sissy," Hymie remarked to Sarah, as chunks of hair drifted to the floor.

Sarah knelt, brushed up some curls, and tucked them in her apron pocket. In what seemed minutes, her baby had become a dark blonde child with a neck so slender; she wondered it would hold his head up. She wiped her eyes and Lindy's on her apron hem.

"Stop your bawling and shake hands." Hymie snatched him off the counter and set him on his feet. "A haircut is a *mitzvah*, son! It means you are a man."

"Yes Pappa," Lindy smiled, with teardrops hanging in his lashes. He put out his small hand.

"Come," Hymie took it. "We will find an ice cream cone to celebrate this *mitzvah*. Chocolate, perhaps?"

Sarah snorted. Pappa was Lindy's favorite—no matter how mean he was. She picked up a rag and began to swipe at bits of hair still sticking to the counter.

***

For Lindy, whose whole world was the tiny store and the cot he shared up in the flat with Nate, his sour, work-pushed father was his only playmate. Pappa had an arm chair, hidden behind a pile of boxes at the back of the store. Whenever he sat down to rest, he had a face made out of the *Jewish Daily Forward*. Cigar smoke drifted up above the paper.

"Play Pappa. Please! Lindy would pester, tapping at the paper with his fingers. Or he'd crawl around the armchair on his hands and knees to tempt his father to play the game of Geezer. Lindy was the little geezer, and Pappa was the big geezer. The big geezer was sly. He'd pretend to be reading the paper. All at once, he'd roll it up between his hands and smack the little geezer on the bottom.

"Ouch!" the little one would yelp. Every time he passed the big geezer, he tried to squirm out of the way. He'd crawl faster and faster, till the floor was burning spots in his bare knees. When he couldn't stand another minute, he'd jump up and run away to hide. Squatting in the closet full of mops and rags, gulping air that smelled of lye, he'd listen to the pounding of his heart. Pretty soon the little geezer would be giggling behind his fist. Then, he'd give a little hint. "Big Geezer. Where are you? Come find me. I'm hi-ding."

Growling, snorting and clumping around the flat, Pappa would call, "Come out you little geezer, or I'm coming in to get you." All of a sudden he'd swoop down on the hiding place. He'd bite Lindy on the neck, tickle him, and cover him with smacking kisses till Lindy almost wet his pants.

"Stop! Help!" He'd gasp so out of breath his throat hurt. It felt scary good. About then, the big geezer would turn back into Pappa and sit down to read the *Jewish Daily Forward*. Lindy had a secret. He was pretty tired by then, too. But he never would have told.

One night, no matter how he teased, Lindy couldn't get his father to play. Finally, Hymie folded his newspaper and laid it down beside his chair. "Come up here." He patted his lap.

Lindy climbed up. He squirmed around. Maybe Pappa was trying out a new game.

"No. Sit Son." His father began rubbing his back. "Talking is the game today. Early in the morning, I will be riding on the streetcar to Montefiore Hospital. The doctor says I need an operation."

Lindy tensed.

Looking him in the eye, Pappa explained that it was a small operation. "Just a little surgery," the doctor had said.

"Will it hurt, Pappa?"

"It will hurt some, they tell me," Pappa said. "I will be coming back home in one-two-three days." He showed Lindy on his fingers. "When I come home, I will be resting. I can't play Geezer right away. I can tell you stories, though. And soon as I am strong again, we can play the Geezer game."

Lindy snuggled into his father's dark blue sweater. "Don't worry, Pappa, I like stories."

"Help your Mamma, Lindy, and be good." Pappa hugged him a little tight. "Three days will go by quickly, I promise."

Before he went to sleep, Lindy explained things to his stuffed dog. "My Pappa will be gone for one-two-three days." He showed the dog on his fingers. "And then he will come back."

The next afternoon, his mother left Aunt Golda and Nate to tend the store. Lindy looked at a book and tossed a ball around. He felt bored and threw the ball at Nathan.

"Hey, cut it out," said Nate. "Can't ya see I gotta work?"

Lindy sat against the wall, gnawing on his thumbnails. All at once, the door slammed back. The door chime clattered on the floor. His mother swept in, sobbing loudly and plucking at the skin on the backs of her hands. Her blouse was ripped partway down the front, and her eyes were flying around. Mrs. Finkel, from next door, and her pregnant daughter were stumbling after her, wringing their hands.

"Sarah, sit!" ordered Mrs. Finkel, grabbing for her skirt. "Troubles you already have, without a broken neck."

"Sister, what is it?" Aunt Golda joined the chase. Her forehead bunched up underneath her hair.

Sarah paced on—bumping into things, yanking out her hairpins and flinging them on the floor, keening, sobbing and muttering to herself. Finally Lindy made out the words.

"Hymie. God! Oh my God! What will I do?"

"Mamma?" Lindy caught her by the wrist.

"Get him out of here," she screamed, jerking backward, "Take him for a walk or something!"

Golda tried to pick him up, but he wriggled away. Running to his mother, he wrapped his arms around her knees and held on tight.

"Mamma," he sobbed. She pried his arms apart and knelt in front of him. Taking his shirt between her fingers, she made a little rip right by the neck. "Your Pappa's dead," she whispered and her eyes burned into him. "His heart stopped! He don't draw breath no more."

Lindy felt her trembling and smelled the stale salt of perspiration. He didn't really know what dead meant. Tracing a finger down a line of tears along her cheek, he spoke softly. "Don't worry, Mamma. My Pappa will be coming back. He promised. He will tell me stories. We will play the game of Geezer, and I will hide." He stroked her face and patted her springy hair. Her keening was so shrill it pierced his ears.

Lindy counted one-two-three days on his fingers. Then he counted four and five. That was as far as fingers went. He watched the neighbors bring in food, and set it on the front room table. He ate when someone told him to, although he wasn't hungry. Below the window on the street, he overheard the passers-by reading a sign someone had tacked up: *Lindy's grocery, closed till further notice for a death in the family.*

Standing in the front room door, Lindy listened to the Rabbi and the men from *shul* chanting *Kaddish*. The men wore *yarmulkes,* and the fringes on their prayer shawls moved as they swayed to and fro. Their chanting was the saddest song Lindy had ever heard. They stood in front of folding chairs and never even sat. Lindy wondered why the chairs were there at all.

Leaning up against the doorframe, he cried with his fist in his mouth. Light and shadow, shape and color, moved in rhythm with the mournful chanting. Through a shiny fog of tears, the men looked as if they were behind the filmy curtain with his father, in the world where spirits go.

On the fifth day, when he ran out of fingers, Lindy had an idea. "I will hide," he told himself. "My Pappa will come and find me. He promised."

Slowly, he walked toward the closet with the mops and brooms, the buckets and rags, and the sharp smell of lye. He slid his back along the wall till he was squatting, and listened to his heart beat. It felt friendly in there. Finally he called out, "Big Geezer. Where are you? Come find me. I'm hi-ding."

He listened for the clomp of boots, the snorts, the booming laugh, and the deep big-geezer growl, "Come out of there, you Little Geezer or I'll come in and get you... "

In the evening, when dusk gathered outside the window, Lindy would go hide in the closet. At first he would sing out, "Pappa, where are you? Come find me. I'm hiding." Finally he stopped calling, and then he stopped talking much at all. But every day near suppertime, he went in and squatted by the wall, hugging his knees with slender arms. And he rocked forward and back, a gray little boy in the dusky shadows, to and fro like the men who chanted *Kaddish* for his father.

Now You Are A Man

"When the father passes to the other side, the son must be a man," Mamma told Nathan the day his father died on the operating table. Pappa arrived at the cemetery in a pine box covered with a fringed *tallit*. The Rabbi snipped the tassel from each corner, pronouncing Hyman Joseph Lindenberg free now of all earthly obligations. The knotted fringes dangled from his fist.

They buried Pappa in a hole cut through the March-brown grass, under shovelfuls of soil laced with ice, laced with mud—without spring flowers to put on the grave. Nate had thought about laying a *challah* on that raw mound of earth, or maybe even a cake. It seemed like Pappa needed something.

Afterwards, his mother dug her fingers in the dirt, and smeared it on her face and hair. Through the long week of mourning, she sat s*hivah* on a low box in the darkened kitchen till the air inside the closed-up flat grew heavy with her moaning. To Nathan, she looked like an ancient crone, rocking and muttering prayers that sounded more like curses. Over and over, little Lindy scrambled up on her lap and touched her face.

She stared at him from eyes burned dry and never moved or raised her arms to hold him.

Every morning Aunt Golda came over with a pot of oatmeal. She'd spoon it into Mamma while Nate spooned it into Lindy. "When *shivah* is over," Golda had promised, "your Mamma will be a Mamma again."

She was—a little. At least she washed her face and hands. She set the wooden box out on the stoop. In an old frayed bathrobe and Pappa's wool socks, she sat up on a chair now, and sipped a glass of tea. Her words, when they came from her mouth, smelled of stale cigarettes.

"Your Pappa was all the time bragging how you're so smart. Making plans for college." She shrugged. "So? Times change. Your father, of blessed memory, can't send no money from the other world. You gotta quit school and help me in the store, Nate."

"Yes, Mamma," he said aloud, and the voice in his head whispered, "No." His mother was a taut-faced stranger.

One evening, Nate had glanced through her half-closed bedroom door and seen her, plucking the hairs out of her head one by one between two fingers, and dropping them into a milk bottle. All the while, she was talking to herself. Nate couldn't make out the words. The black hairs were growing to a springy pile inside the bottle. He walked to his room and closed the door to keep the strangeness out.

Afterwards, he lay awake thinking what to do. His little brother Lindy was snuggled up against his chest, snoring lightly with the tears he'd cried to sleep. Is this a life? Nate wondered. Memories of things that would be no more passed before him like movie film—afternoon ball games on the IKS playground, the tautness of his body poised to shoot a basket, his friend's faces, Miller school and the smells of ink and newsprint in the office of the weekly *Owl*. He'd never be editor now.

Maybe he would see Mac Rabinowitz again. Mac quit school awhile ago. Nate had run into him hauling produce from the incline to the fruit market in a wagon with a broken down old horse. Mac pulled up the reins and grinned around a toothpick. "You ain't seen me around much—my Pappa's not so good. I am responsible for the economics in the family now. Got me a business ... long as this old horse don't die." Mac didn't let things get him down. Instead he went to school at night. Now there was an idea.

The half moon cast a patch of light on the bedroom wall. Nate tucked the covers around Lindy. His brother's back was as warm and bony as kitten. Nathan yawned. His eyes drifted closed.

In his dream, he was standing in the front doorway, squinting at the kitchen through a foggy wall. His father's body was laid out on the kitchen table, the prayer shawl pulled clear to his chin. Two feet poked up at the bottom then bony knees, and a knobby pile of folded hands. Pappa's face, above the shroud, was absolutely still. Long lashes rested soft against his cheeks. A shadow, swift as a match flicker, moved across the lashes and pricked in Nathan's throat. He winced, drew a breath and held it. His father's eyelids fluttered up; he raised himself up on his arms and flung his feet over the edge of the table. Black shoes tapped the wooden floor and Pappa stood. He pulled off his *yarmulke*, moved a hand over his rumpled hair, and set it back atop his head.

Dybbuk, thought Nate, and turned to run. "Shalom my son," his father spoke in a voice as normal as Friday. When he reached through the door to take Nate's hand, the fog scattered into threads and disappeared. Across the kitchen and over to the window, he led Nate. They stood there looking at the sky. To the left, the sun was dropping toward the horizon. A new moon was rising on the right.

"Quickly," Pappa gave Nate a little shove. "We must make Sabbath before the sun is down." He took the *tallit* by two corners and spread it over the table like a cloth. He and Nathan found candlesticks, two new candles, half a loaf of challah from the bread box, a crystal decanter of wine, two glasses.

"Boruch Atoh Adonoi Eloheinu, Melech Ha-o'lom," they chanted.

Pappa lit the candles. Through the carafe of sweet grape wine, their flames cast shadows like spattered blood across the white silk shawl.

"A memorable Sabbath," the father said, kissing Nathan on both cheeks. His breath was warm as life. "Please to listen carefully. These words must last a lifetime. Never again will you hear my voice, till you reach the other side."

With his tawny hair and his mouth smiling down at Nathan, Pappa looked striking. He dropped his hands, moved to the window and pushed it wide. Nathan watched him stretch an arm high into the night, and pull the crescent moon down from the sky.

Nate wrapped his arms around himself and held on tight to keep collected. His father was undoing the buttons on his shirt. As he drew the crescent blade over his skin, a patch of golden hairs gleamed on his pale chest. Ruby droplets oozed along the edges of the cut.

Pappa chanted all the while, a low and haunting melody that Nate had never heard—yet he joined in. Dipping his fingers in the blood, the father laid his hand on Nathan's heart. "Take care of Mamma, Son," he murmured. "She's not too strong.

"And be a pappa for your little brother. You got to be a man now."

Pappa's palm was warm on Nathan's chest. Tears sprung from the corners of Nate's eyes and trickled down his nose. His father held his shoulders and they danced then, round and round the table, their voices blending deep and high—round the kitchen past the window, where the strip of dark sky was growing lighter, growing pale.

Shreds of dreams floated to the ceiling and blew away like mist. Nathan opened his eyes and lay completely still. A fat fly buzzed against the window. Outside, a crescent moon was fading in a pale blue wash of morning light. The smell of ammonia stung his nostrils. Lindy wet the bed. The sheets were stuck to Nathan's legs.

Pappa had died on the table. "I don't understand it," the doctor had said. "There wasn't any reason for his heart to stop." Nate couldn't figure why the doctor let it happen. His chest hurt. A raw place over his heart stung every time he drew a breath, almost as if he, not Pappa, had had surgery.

Climbing out of bed, Nate tucked the blankets around Lindy and pulled on the pants he'd dropped the night before. Five-thirty—too late to go say *Kaddish* for his Pappa, although Nate was a man now, and big enough to say it. Time to get ready and go to work.

Mamma was asleep with her head on the kitchen table. The fingers of one hand lay in her ashtray full of half-smoked cigarettes. Nate picked up the hand and moved it over to the side. She groaned a little.

He poured himself a glass of tea and accidently kicked it over, while he was tying his boots. The key was hanging on a nail by the kitchen door. Nate took it down. Slowly, he tramped down the flight of stairs he'd always run before. Cliff Street was waking up. Peddlers hollered greetings to each other, drinking mugs of tea and setting out their wares. Men wandered by on their way home from praying at the synagogue. Freshly combed children, with water in their hair and notebooks on their arms, hurried along to school. The iceman balanced a twenty-five pound block in his tongs and pounded on a tenement door.

Nate turned his back on Cliff Street, fit the key into the latch, and stepped into *Lindy's* dimness.

The Black Hand

"One dollar will be the glasses," Yossel, the optician, said to Lindy's Mamma as he bent the wire pieces to fit over Lindy's ears. Then, grasping the frames at the corners, he pressed them down over the little boy's nose. Lindy flinched.

"Lookit me!" Yossel flicked him on the forehead, then glanced uneasily at Sarah.

Lindy raised his eyes to Yossel's face. For five years, his whole world been a blur. Now the optician's nose was mushy red, a strawberry peppered with tiny black pits. Two wiry hairs poked from one nostril. Lindy almost plucked one, then looked embarrassed at the floor. His shoes jumped up at him—scuffed brown leather with frayed laces tied in double bows. A scab on his left knee was frilly at the edges. He stuck his thumbnail underneath and pulled. With things suddenly so big and sharp, Lindy felt bewildered. Yanking off the glasses, he ground his knuckles in his eyes. His feet went back to the familiar fuzzy distance.

"A whole dollar you should be ashamed to charge a widow for two pieces of glass," His mamma complained. "*Shah*, Yossel! You are a thief."

Once more Lindy set the glasses on his nose, tucked the curved wires around his ears. Glancing sideways, he caught the glint of gold frames. His sight was trapped behind the two glass circles. In order to see right or left, he had to turn his head.

"What use for my baby to see from his eyes if he has to die from starvation?" his mother's voice ground on. "Glasses are not useful to a dead person, don't you agree Mr. Yossel?" Luckily, Lindy's ears still worked the old way.

Lindy inspected the backs of his hands. His veins were faint blue tracings on skin as thin as tissue paper. As he studied his hands, he thought of the latest poster in the display case outside the New Granada Theater. A huge black hand was poking out of a stormy purple sky. Its nails were long and curled forward like claws. Two silver lightning bolts zigzagged across the sky. Below them, twelve letters, T-h-e B-l-a-c-k H-a-n-d, dripped bright red drops of blood. Lindy bent his fingers to a claw. It wasn't too convincing with the fingernails all bitten off. He bet the Black Hand never chewed its nails.

The glasses pinched behind his ears. He tucked his fingers under the wires and massaged in little circles. While he was rubbing, his thoughts turned to a few nights ago when he was jumping on the bed by Nathan's head. Shrill with glee, he bounced from knees to feet and down again.

"Cut it out, Lind." Nate grabbed him by the ankle, and Lindy landed with a thump.

"Know what, Pipsqueak? The Black Hand is in this room right now." Pinned below his brother on the mattress, Lindy felt Nate's fingernails graze his neck. His forehead started sweating. Nathan's lips hung toward him in the dimness.

His nails dug into the back of Lindy's neck.

Lindy lay as still as Pappa in his coffin, his heart thumping so hard it filled the room. No matter what, he'd never let his brother know-how scared he was.

"Sarah," Yossel's whiny voice brought Lindy back. "I, too, have mouths to feed: my mamma, four children, two great aunts. Go, please, to the Jewish Free Loan Society, and see if they will give you money for the glasses. One week I will wait. If necessary, a little longer."

The bickering was giving Lindy a stomach ache. He wandered to a frame display, set his glasses on the shelf and tried another pair. Standing on tiptoe, he squinted in the yellowed mirror. The frames were for a grown-up. The hollow black circles made him look like one of the raccoons who rummaged through the garbage piles at night.

Lindy was bored. A strip of light at the back of the store led him to a door ajar. He pushed on it and slipped into the alley. He'd just stay out a little while. He didn't want trouble when Mamma finally did decide to leave.

Pools of daylight spilled into his glasses. When his eyes adjusted, Lindy stared in wonder at a world he'd never seen. Sunshine trickled through the clotheslines that crisscrossed the alley between the tenements. Pieces of wash had different shapes. A large pair of striped undershorts was hanging right above him. He caught a whiff of rotting garbage. Hills of stinking debris lined both sides of the alley: rusty cans, jagged pieces of glass that glinted in the sun, discarded boxes, torn clothing, and soot. The walls were thick with it. Words were scrawled across the bricks in coal black letters. Lindy wished that he could read. Bricks were rough—he hadn't noticed that before—with grayish stuff between. He traced his finger along a groove and followed it down the alley till it ended at Cliff Street.

Pushcarts and people jammed the street. Men threw spotted dice on street corners and children darted in between. Peddlers sat on stools or folding chairs, or against walls, hawking piles of brooms and mops. The colors were so bright he had to close his eyes. Bumping along with the crowd, straining tall to see into the distance, he made a marvelous discovery. Over the cliffs at the end of the neighborhood, he spied the shiny strip of river where he and Nathan sometimes swam on hot days. He could hardly wait for summer. He pictured himself holding his nose, drifting to the cool green bottom, standing up with water slipping down his skin.

Ahead of him on Cliff Street, rough voices singled themselves out into words. Three big boys swaggered up, puffing on stogies.

"Well if it ain't," one growled, looming over Lindy. He wore a checkered porkpie hat.

"Ain't what'?" asked the fat one in the middle.

"Ain't the littlest *Kike* I ever seen. Got four eyes too."

So quickly Lindy had no time to squeak, two of them grabbed him under the armpits, lifted his feet off the ground, and forced him back into the empty alley. "Jew-boy, eh?" The third one poked him in the ribs. "Ain't ya?" The finger jabbed his chest again. Through the glasses, Lindy noticed scraggly black whiskers and reddish-purple bumps with gooey yellow tops.

"Ain't either!" stammered Lindy. Nate and Mac had warned him about guys like this. Too bad they hadn't told him what to do.

"Hey kiddo, this is our lucky day. We're out lookin' fer Jews to cut. Already got a whole collection." The guy pulled out a pen knife out and pried open the blade with his dirty thumbnail. "You better prove it quick you ain't a *kike*."

A hand darted out and yanked at Lindy's knickers. The buttons popped and rolled along the ground. Lindy stooped and grabbed for his pants. A foot shot out and toppled him. "Leave em where they are."

"Stand up damnit." A boot struck his other hip. Lindy let the pants go and stumbled to his feet. The three broke into loud guffaws.

"Ain't that the about the littlest pecker you ever seen?"

"See that little hole in the tip, bare naked with no skin around it? That proves you're a Jewboy. No question about it. Don't you know that holes s'posed to be covered up with nice clean foreskin?"

Four skins? The big boy made as if to flick it. Lindy felt his penis cringe and tucked his hand over it. The porkpie smacked his hand away. Cold pinpricks moved up Lindy's thighs, his stomach, and his chest. He shivered. He'd never felt so naked in his life. If only he could faint, like Aunt Golda during hay fever season when she couldn't get her breath.

All at once the alley dwindled to the size and sharp-edged clarity of a picture in a frame. Light glinted on a partly open window in the wall above. A cast iron pot cooled on the sill and curtains moved a little in the air. Lindy was in the picture too, standing with his pants down, their useless' straps splayed out across the gravel. Beside his brown shoes lay a red and white Dentyne wrapper, a dirty penny and a broken yellow pencil.

"It's such a puny little thing, hardly worth bothering with." A calloused thumb and finger were measuring the length and width of his penis. A hand was squeezing, pulling, fingers grabbing at the little sac underneath. The porkpie hat was right by Lindy's chest. It had a little button in the middle. At the sound of groaning, he looked up and saw the fat guy jerking frantically at the front of his pants.

Trying to keel over, Lindy held his breath until the edges of the world blurred. But he couldn't make it go away.

"Cut it out, George," the third guy ordered a long time later. "Can't you see there ain't no sense wasting it. It's gotta grow a couple more years."

"A couple more inches too," the fat one laughed. "It might get lost in the collection." Lindy pictured stacked up shoeboxes, each one filled to the brim with penises. He wished he had a baseball bat to smash the big guys' heads until they were squirting blood and their eyes bugged out. And their teeth were broken and they couldn't even whisper, 'cause they were dead. He forced his breathing to slow, then knelt and reached for his pants.

"Cut it ..." A forearm banged his chest.

"Let 'im go, Jack. Didn't we decide he ain't a keeper?"

Lindy wrapped his straps around his stomach and tied a lumpy knot.

"Tell ya what. We'll turn our backs, you little prick, and give you ten to run like hell."

"One-two-three... "

Holding onto his knickers, Lindy ducked between two buildings. A privy stood at the back of the space. Its door hung crooked from a single leather thong. Lindy stepped inside, pulled the door shut, and yanked the latch until it caught. The stink flooded into his nostrils.

The boys' coarse voices faded down the alley. Lindy waited a few minutes to be sure they were gone. Then he pulled the latch. Stuck? Breathing through his mouth, he pulled again. Stuck! The latch jiggled and clicked, but it wouldn't budge.

Light slanted between the planks. "Help," he called. His head was spinning and his stomach hurt. Surely at least one person would pass before it got dark. "Somebody help me!" The privy was nearly hidden between two buildings. Lindy swallowed spit to save his voice. He wouldn't waste it until he really heard someone.

Sooner or later, Nate would miss him, wouldn't he? Lindy closed his eyes and concentrated on poking silent calls for help into his brother's ears. Besides, if he wasn't in bed by the time Mamma finished at the store, she'd make Nate go out and look for him. "Don't worry, Lindy," he kept telling himself.

Hours passed. Shadows climbed the privy walls. Once, Lindy heard footsteps in the alley. "Nathan. Somebody!" he yelled. The footsteps faded. Once he'd started screaming though, Lindy couldn't stop. He hollered until his throat was raw, and he had to breathe the stink in through his nose. It clung inside his nostrils and burned his eyes. Finally, he squeezed them shut.

Something moved inside the privy, scratched across the splintery walls. Rats? Lindy's eyes popped open. Fingers moved over his head, his hair. He jumped back against the door. Right in front of him, poking out of the one holer, groping around at the end of an arm that stretched long and longer, was The Black Hand. Lindy shook his head. He wiped his glasses on his shirt and put them on again. Still the hand was there. Lindy knew the monster's body lurked behind it—its other hairy arm, its teeth. Oh God! Without taking his eyes off the hand, he reached behind him and yanked the latch with all his strength. It didn't budge. His knees were weak and shook so hard he had to squat. He couldn't help it. The hand was reaching out to grab him, and drag his little body through the hole into all that poop and pee and night soil.

Inhaling the putrid air, Lindy lay down on the floor and sobbed until he vomited.

***

"Lindy, Lind, for God sakes where are you?" The cracks were completely dark.

"Lindy," the voices grew louder, frantic. His brother and his best friend, Mac.

"Lindy, yell for God sakes! Yell as loud as you can."

"Nay-dee," Lindy pushed his voice up through tangles of tears and snot. He pounded his fists on the splintery walls.

"Over here," he croaked over and over, afraid they'd leave and he would die for sure. "In the privy."

Then the boys were right outside. They jiggled the bolt and yanked, jerking the handle till the old boards snapped. The door swung open on its leather hinge. Choking and blubbering, Lindy stumbled out and threw himself against Nate's brown jacket.

"Goddamn, you stink!" Nate pushed him backward. "What the hell have you been doing?"

As hard as he tried, Lindy couldn't stop crying. He felt ashamed in front of Mac and Nathan. His brother's penis was big enough to cut ... big enough to make the collection. He hated the new glasses, all smeared and blurry now, that helped him see the big boys hands, the knife, the black hand, the whole shameful deformed mess of things that day. Pulling them off, he threw them on the ground. Then he picked them up, wiped them on his shirt, and shoved them in his pocket.

Nate and Mac led him down Cliff Street and over the bluff to the river. Gathering sticks and pieces of a wooden crate, they got a bonfire going.

"Awright, Lindy. Time for a bath," Nate dropped a pile of sticks beside the fire and rolled his pants above his knees. Then, snatching Lindy up under one arm, he strode down to the river bank, through the weeds and brush, right into the water. Lindy yelped and wriggled, but he couldn't escape. Nathan dropped him in the water, clothes and all. By the time he'd sputtered to the surface, his pants and shirt were floating on the water. Holding Lindy by the neck, Nate rubbed him all over with a handful of sand, even in his hair. Grains of it stung his eyes, and his skin bumped up like chicken flesh. He bellowed till his breath ran out, then settled down to whimpering.

"Awright, awright!" Nate let go, and Lindy scrambled up the river bank, shaking with the cold.

Nate slipped off his jacket. "Here, put this on and sit beside the fire." Nate sat and pulled Lindy down beside him. Stiff all over, with water dripping down his

111

chest and soaking Nathan's jacket, Lindy moaned a single note through chattering teeth.

Mac piled driftwood on the fire. He lit a cigarette from a flaming stick and handed one to Nathan. The pile of sticks crackled and blazed up, warming Lindy's cheeks and forehead. On a flat rock next to the fire, his shoes began to steam.

Mac stood and began digging in his pockets. Three brown potatoes dropped to the ground and rolled in front of Nate and Lindy.

"Stay around this guy, little brother," Nathan laughed. "The police might get you, but you won't go hungry."

Lindy looked skeptical. He had heard the story of how Mac had trained the cat to watch over him, while Nate and Mac played basketball.

Mac bowed so low his cap fell off his head and covered up the three potatoes. When he picked it up, there were only two. "See Lind, it's easy. Wanna try?" He turned the cap over to show the potato underneath. "Drop your hat on Leon's produce wagon. Plenty for everyone—oranges, onions, and pears. Today we have fresh potatoes. He sounded like a pushcart vendor. After scraping the coals together, he set the three potatoes on the glowing pile. Every few minutes, he turned them with a fat stick. Snuggled between Nathan's knees, Lindy slipped his pants on. They were almost dry. His hair had finally stopped dripping. His brother's skin was warm against his back as the story came out between sobs.

"Listen, Lindy. Worse things happen than getting stuck in an old privy. Worse than those guys picking on you too. Lots worse. People die, Lindy. Nobody died. If no one dies, things can always get better." Nathan's voice was earnest.

Mac took up the cause. "We have potatoes and a pocket full of salt." He licked a finger, dipped it in his pocket and stuck it in Lindy's mouth. It tasted sharp and watery.

"Look!" Mac pointed at the sky.

Lindy slipped his glasses on. The lenses were like telescopes. He'd never seen the stars before. Not this way—sharp against the velvet sky, like diamonds.

"There's the Big Dipper," His eyes followed Mac's finger. "It's like a pan. See? With a bent handle. That blazing star, right on the end?"

Lindy nodded.

"That's the North Star. Explorers used to navigate by it. When I was your size Lindy, I walked across Russia with Mamma and Pappa... to escape. That was when we came to America. Every night that star was up there."

Lindy was getting drowsy. The big boys' voices murmured on. Their cigarette tips glowed orange in the dark. A sweet charred smell rose up from the potatoes. Then Mac was digging with his stick, cutting the potatoes with his knife. "Here," he held a chunk by Lindy's mouth. 'Blow on it. It's hot."

Charred on the outside, steamy-soft in the middle, the potato tasted fresh as milk. Chewing, Lindy raised a hand and touched his brother's cheek. Downy hair was growing below Nathan's temples. Lindy stroked it gently, remembering in some dark place that had no words, his father's rougher beard.

The Passover Bunny

Lindy sat in Mrs. Hager's third grade classroom getting a sore throat again. The swollen tonsils and the pricking in his ears each time he swallowed made it hard to concentrate.

OUR DAILY NEWS, May 2, 1918, Mrs. Hager printed on the blackboard in round white letters. Lindy copied the words across the top of his blue-lined tablet with a newly sharpened pencil. The iron radiator hissed steam. Too warm, Lindy, slipped out of his seat, moved to the window on his left, and grunted as he pushed it open. A breeze caressed his hot cheeks and forehead. It blew across his forearms and his desk-top with its pencil groove, and fluffed the pages of his tablet.

The sky was pale as laundry starch, and tight buds covered the catalpa tree outside. "Close the window, Lindy," snapped Mrs. Hager. "That wind is going to give someone pneumonia."

His mouth drew into a tight line—just his usual bad luck. Lindy thought a lot about his life. To begin with, he had bad eyes and glasses thick as bottle bottoms. Stickball was impossible because he couldn't see the ball. Worse yet, his tonsils were a mess.

He was always getting sick. So he had to take cod liver oil and put up with Aunt Golda's hot stinking mustard plasters on his chest and neck. The doctor said the tonsils had to come out. He said it would be just a little surgery. Lindy knew about just a little surgery. His father had died of it. "A little surgery," the doctor had said, and a clot had traveled through Pappa's bloodstream to his heart.

He never even came home from the hospital—he went to the Jewish cemetery, instead. That was when Lindy's mother turned into a gray rag of a person who was always saying, "Lindy, ask your brother. I don't have time." She limped and *kvetched* and smelled of cigarettes and her own sweat. Lindy didn't look into her eyes anymore, because when he did, he ached as though her heart were breaking inside his chest.

From the day the doctor mentioned surgery, Lindy never again let on when he was sick. He planned to keep his tonsils till he died. That was why he never missed a day of school. Besides that, he loved school. To read about America, to dip strips of newspaper in flour and water paste and pinch them into mountains on a map of Pennsylvania, to win the weekly spelling bee— filled him with excitement. He didn't even mind copying

OUR DAILY NEWS from the blackboard every morning, even though his handwriting was already excellent.

"Who has an item for Daily?" Mrs. Hager stood poised at the board, a piece of chalk between her fingers. Several hands went up.

"The fire wagon came last night!" Chana Levich was practically bursting. "The sirens screeched so awful, I had to put my fingers in my ears. An old man dropped his stogie and set the rug on fire."

Chalk scratched on the blackboard. Heads nodded over tablets. Hands formed letters into words.

"Lucky for us, somebody was drinking a glass of water, and threw it at the burning place," breathed Chana. "Otherwise we might be sitting in the street with nothing. The firemen never even had to screw their hoses on the hydrant."

Lindy brought a want ad. "Wanted!" he read, careful to pronounce the words without a trace of greenhorn, "Good ideas for things to purchase for five cents. Third grade boy wants to buy something special with a buffalo nickel that has been burning a hole in his pocket since Chanukah. Please contact Sidney Lindenberg (Lindy)"

"Hey Lindy." Joey Rizzo pulled him over to the spiked iron fence at recess. "Funny you should mention yer nickel. I got five cents too. A peddler down on

Center is selling chocolate Easter Rabbits. Ten cents. Wanna go in on one?"

"Well...maybe," Lindy hesitated. Joey could be a bit of a *shyster*.

"They're this big." Joe spread his palms apart. "The sign says solid milk chocolate. They're light brown—not that coal black bitter kind. Maybe we could talk him down to eight cents."

Lindy was tempted. Chocolate was his favorite food, except for ice cream. Then he remembered *Pesach*. The first Seder was tonight.

"Sorry Joe, I can't do it. Passover starts at sunset. It's a Jewish holiday. I have to eat special food for eight whole days. No this, no that. You know, especially no candy from a pushcart." The thought of disobeying Pesach filled Lindy's heart with solemn dread.

Joey bit his lip. "No problem Lindy! We'll just go ahead and buy it. I'll take it home and save it till your Holy Days are done."

"I guess it might be OK to take a look," Lindy tried to be tentative.

After school, he stopped home for his Hebrew book. Then he ran by Joey's, and the two of them headed for the pushcart district. Sandwiching their way among overflowing tables, peddlers with frying pans and rakes, rows of pushcarts and human beings of every shape and age, they spotted the chocolate bunnies lined up at the front of a wobbly old pushcart. A sign tacked to the front read, *Solid Chocolate Easter Bunnies! Limited supply. 10 cents apiece.* Each rabbit was a perfect likeness, right down to the whiskers and a nose that looked as if it might start twitching any second.

"Wow! I bet they're a foot tall," Joey exclaimed. Lindy didn't need convincing. He'd been sold the minute he saw them. The peddler looked about as rickety as his pushcart. A purplish groove ran up his cheek and around one eye like a monocle. The eye moved, as if it could see, but slanted downward toward his cheek. A miniature yarmulke, trimmed in silver braid, sat atop his mousy hair. Lindy wondered how a Jewish peddler came by Easter bunnies just in time for Pesach. He hoped the peddler wasn't a friend of his mother's. She would say the bunny was a piece of *schlock.*

The boys squeezed in front of the pushcart.

"Give ya five cents for a rabbit," Joey called.

"For ten inches solid chocolate? You insult me."

"We got the money," Lindy explained. "How do we know for sure they ain't hollow? Can I pick one up?" He reached.

The peddler thwacked his hand. "You buy, you don't buy, it's all the same to me.

See the sign? *Limited supply.* I don't need your business."

"Don't look too limited to me," Joe muttered under his breath. The boys stared at each other, trying to talk in sentences with their eyes.

"*Gay Avek*, you two. Let someone up here who won't waste my time."

Five minutes before Lindy was supposed to leave for *Cheder*, they handed over their nickels. The peddler tucked the rabbit in a paper bag and handed it to Joey.

"Don't eat it all at once," he said.

Lindy was having trouble leaving. "Do you think we maybe ought to test it?"

"Definitely!" Joe nodded. "It could be hollow or something." He pulled the rabbit out of the bag and held it by its ears.

Chocolate fragrance swirled around their heads. For a moment they wavered, reluctant to mar the perfect rabbit shape with human teeth. And then they bit the toes off.

"Mmmm," Lindy was drooling for another bite. He thought about playing hooky from Hebrew, and eating his whole half before *Pesach* began at sunset. But he didn't want the *Rabbi* sending Mamma an absent note. "I gotta go now, Joe. I'm late already, and Reb Zelner spanks for tardy." His feet were sticking to the sidewalk. "Joe?"

"Aw, c'mon Lind. You worried I'll eat it? I promised, okay?"

"I just wish you were Jewish. That's all. Then you couldn't eat it either, till Passover was done."

"Who'd we get to keep it for us then?" Joey asked reasonably. "Look Nathan."

He raised his right hand and touched two fingers to his forehead, his heart, and both sides of his chest. "Cross my heart and hope to die, Lindy, if I break my promise." Then he raised his hand toward the sky. "And raise my hand to God."

Lindy left Joey with his hand still sticking in the air. Twirling his tongue around the melting chocolate toes, he stumbled. His Hebrew book flew up and hit the muddy street.

He wiped the book on his knickers, kissed it, and raced on, until he almost collided with the heavy double doors of the *Irene Kaufmann Settlement*.

He tore cross the lobby, past the athletic trophies in their two glass cases, and up three flights of stairs. Pausing at the classroom door, Lindy pulled a yarmulke out from his pocket and slipped it on. Then he poked his head around the door and ducked into an empty seat in back. Anchel Cohen, next to him, pointed out the page.

"Sidney Joseph Lindenberg!" thundered the *Reb*. "Perhaps you have some pressing business that is keeping you from coming on time to *Cheder*?"

"No Sir. I'm sorry, Sir." He hung his head.

"Come up here."

Reb Zelner smelled of garlic and damp wool. He grabbed Lindy by the wrist, spun him around and gave him two hard swats on the behind. Lindy didn't feel a thing.

***

Zayde Ezra arranged two cushions in an armchair, pulled it to the Seder table, and sat. He gestured Lindy to the chair at his right. Zayde was a *Cohen* and *Talmud Jew*. When he was young, he'd been a chicken *shohet* for a *shul* in Riga. He still koshered chickens. But now he was shabby and smelled of old man. Tufts of steel-wool hair poked below his blue embroidered *yarmulke*. His gnarled fingers trembled as he opened his *Hagaddah*. What Lindy could see of Zayde's neck was mottled as a turkey. Lindy stroked the smoothness of his own neck. Old was awful. He decided he would never get old.

Mamma pulled a crocheted shawl up over her gray hair. Its point hung down below her waist. Striking a blue-tipped sulfur match, she lit two candles standing tall in silver holders. Aunt Golda, in a concert dress of light green fluff, stood by Mamma's elbow like a taller twin. *"Boruch Atoh Adonoi, Eloheinu, Melech Ha'olom."*

The women chanted. The candles smelled of warm wax. Their flames jumped in the silverware.

Holding up a plate with three square matzos wrapped in a linen napkin, Zayde spoke the age old words that open every *seder* in the world, *This is the bread of affliction that our ancestors ate in Egypt. Let all those who are hungry, enter and eat thereof, and all who are in distress, come and celebrate the Passover.* His fringed *tallit* was so enormous, it unfurled like a bird wing.

Lindy's brother, Nathan, sat across from him, handsome in a pressed white shirt and tie, his narrow *tallit* light against his jacket. For this night, he'd even cleaned his fingernails. Above Nate's upper lip, he wore a new blonde moustache. He kept twitching his nose, rabbit-like, as though it tickled.

"And now," Zayde poked him in the shoulder, "If the youngest son can take the time from his important daydreaming, we will have the four questions."

"Mah Nishtanu Halailoh Hazeh," Lindy read from his *Hagaddah.* He would always be the youngest, unless his mother found a husband and had a baby boy. "Why is this night different from all other nights?" He translated. An answer flashed in his mind's eyes like letters on a banner, *Because there is a solid chocolate Easter Bunny, waiting for me in Joey Rizzo's flat.*

The Seder dragged for hours. Lindy's mind meandered in and out. As he ate *charoseth*, tart with apples, raisins, nuts and honey; as he dipped his fluffy stalk of parsley in salt water to honor thousands of years of Jewish tears; as he broke a piece of matzo and spread it with bitter horseradish; imaginary chocolate swirled in the air around him and the flavor on his tongue was sweet.

Zayde Ezra began calling out the names of the ten plagues. "Blood, frogs, vermin, locusts... slaying of the firstborn son."

Lindy dipped his finger in his wineglass. One by one, he dripped the plagues out on his plate. They ran together in a crimson puddle.

This was his favorite part of the *seder*. When it came to taking care of the Jews, Jehovah didn't mess around. In fact, He was so powerful that he could separate the sea to make a path, then sweep it back and drown the Egyptian warriors· in their chariots.

Lindy sucked the last drop off his finger—the skin around the nail was stained purple. At last he got so drowsy he had to push his eyelids with his thumbs. A draft blew in the door and startled him awake. Zayde was welcoming the Prophet Elijah, in case he was waiting on the stoop this year to announce the coming of the Messiah. A silver cup of wine had been poured for him. Lindy had always been curious how Elijah could drink all the wine in one neighborhood, let alone on every *seder* table in the world, even if he only took a tiny sip at every home.

"Come, little brother," Nathan's hands dropped on his shoulders. "You've already had a little too much *Manischewitz*. You are sleeping on the table." He pulled the chair out, lifted Lindy, and deposited him on his cot in the next room. Hands undid the buttons of his shirt, folded it, and pulled his knickers off. The featherbed slid up his legs, his chest, and stopped under his chin. When Nathan bent to say good night, he caught a whiff of *Barbasol*.

Lindy peered into the dimness. A life-sized rabbit hopped across the room on chocolate feet. They thumped because they had no toes.

***

That eight days of *Pesach* was the longest week of Lindy's life. Outside Mrs. Hager's window the catalpa buds opened into pink and white clusters, and began dropping on the street. Several times, the teacher caught him daydreaming. She kept him after school one day, and asked if anything was wrong.

"No." Lindy shook his head, and stayed inside his fancy. His night dreams were so full of chocolate, he sometimes woke up queasy.

Every noon, he checked with Joe at recess. "Hey, Joe. How's our bunny?"

"Good, Lind. The bunny's good.

"You hid it in a safe place, right? Not where your brothers can find it."

"Under the washtub. Way back in a bunch of junk."

"Don't eat it Joe. OK?"

"Of course not, Lindy. I crossed my heart, didn't I?" After awhile, Joe began to sound offended.

Lindy struggled to be patient. When he was absolutely honest with himself, he knew he'd sneak at least one bite if he were Joey. He hoped his friend had stronger will power than he did.

***

It wasn't till years later, when the rift was healed, and they both were almost men that Joey told him what had happened during that long week. Joey slept with his two brothers in the kitchen, on a couch made bigger by three chairs, and covered over with a featherbed. He'd put the rabbit's paper bag beneath the washtub, between the soap, a bag of clothespins and the washboard. The first night, as he drifted off, a soft whispery rabbit voice started calling to him. "Jo-ey. Jo-ey."

He sat straight up in bed.

"Jo-ey. Take me out and have a bite."

Joe squeezed his eyes closed and put his fingers in his ears. Finally he slipped out of bed, tiptoed across the room, lay flat on his belly, and stuck his hand under the washtub. He inched the bag toward him, so as not to wake his brothers. In the dark, he checked the bunny. He ran a finger along its ears, its nose. The downturned groove of mouth was closed. He fingered Lindy's tooth marks and his own. He really ought to take a little bite out of each foot, he reasoned, right above where they had bitten. Just to keep the rabbit quiet.

Joey longed to take second bite. Instead, he crossed his heart twice, shoved the bunny back under the washtub, and crawled under the quilt beside his brothers. The next night, the whispering was more insistent. "Hey Joe. C'mon, take a bite. Take two. They'll be plenty left for Lindy."

That night, Joe ate the feet and ankles. Just to shut the rabbit up. Maybe he'd tell Lindy his brothers got a hold of it and wrecked it.

"Hey Joe." The rabbit's nagging was getting frantic. "C'mon, Joe. Easter is already over. Chocolate is for eating, not for saving."

Every night Joe had to take a few more bites. He wasn't really lying to Lindy, either—till the sixth night, when he ate both ears, wiped his mouth, and threw away the paper bag.

***

Pesach ended Monday at sunset. Lindy hardly slept all night. On Tuesday, he was squirming in his seat. Mrs. Hager threatened to take him in the cloak room and paddle his bottom to help him settle down. She was explaining the facts of long division. Lindy thought of it in terms of chocolate. If two boys have a ten inch rabbit, each of them will get to eat five inches. He pictured himself walking out the iron gate, past the fence, over the mashed catalpa blooms, and hurrying through the soft spring air to Joey's flat—to his very own five inches of chocolate rabbit. When the bell rang, he was poised to dash. He ran home, grabbed his book, and flew down Cliff Street. "Hi Joe!" He panted. "Get the rabbit. I thought I'd die waiting."

"Hi Lind. How about we find a game of stickball first?"

"Maybe after Hebrew, Joe. Umm, *Pesach* is over—sunset last night. Go get the rabbit now, okay?"

Joey was staring at his feet, kicking up little puffs of dust that sifted back down on his shoes. Lindy stared at Joey's feet too.

"Joey...I have to get to Hebrew."

Silence.

A terrible sinking feeling was filling up the space behind his eyes. "You kept the promise, didn't you?"

"Lind, I don't know quite how to say this but ..." Joey ripped the edge of his thumbnail off. Blood filled up the little groove, and he sucked it. "Lind, it was the damnedest thing. Every night that rabbit called to me, 'Joe, come eat me. Joe, take a bite.' I just couldn't take the pestering, Lind. He made me eat him."

Sure! Lindy thought. Tears burned behind his eyes. He took a ragged breath. He didn't stay to hear the rest, but spun around on lightning feet. Joey was an operator, worse, a *shyster* and a *goniff*. Lindy had known it from the start. How could he have been so stupid? "Never trust the *goyim*!" Golda, Mamma, his brother Nate, even his Pappa had drummed into him since he was small. He'd forgotten all about it. Chest burning, Lindy finally slowed down to a walk. He noticed that he'd run all the way to the river. Smokestacks from the steel mills on the other side choked orange sparks and gobs of smoke into the sky. The river gleamed pale green below the sky.

Leaves and sticks bobbed at the edges, and the mud smelled clean and sharp. Lindy picked a rock up, threw it. Then another, harder, till he was hurling them with all his strength, yelling words into the wind, "Crap! Goddam! Damnit to Hell!"

Finally, his arm ached and he lowered it. Green circles spread across the water. He sat down on a clump of tufted grass, and moisture seeped into his underwear. Breaking off a pussy willow, he popped the furry buds off with his thumb.

The opening words of the *seder* seemed to shimmer on a band of light above the water. "This is the bread of affliction, that our forefathers ate in Egypt ..."

Affliction, that was a good word. It meant bad luck, calamity. Lindy was afflicted with colds and bad tonsils. He was afflicted with cod liver oil and mustard plasters and cupping that burned black rings on his skinny chest. He was afflicted with headaches and bad eyes. And now, he was afflicted with being too chicken to give Joey a bloody nose for breaking his promise. God didn't strike Joe dead after he crossed his heart and hoped to die. He didn't even give him hives or poison ivy! Lindy wanted his nickel back. He wanted his five inches of bunny.

He could hear his *Zayde* calling out the ten plagues in a voice of doom. He pictured the purple drops of wine, falling from his finger. Maybe if he concentrated as hard as he could, Lindy could get the Holy One to send a plague for Joey Rizzo. Not as bad as killing a first son. More like making his pee turn to blood, or having the chocolate bites inside him turn into rabbit with brown fur, and a beating heart, and claws to scratch away at Joey's insides.

Irish Mist

A few months after Pappa died, they lost the store. The repossessors came and packed up everything, down to half a jug of lye and a butter scoop with a cracked handle. Afterwards, Nate pushed a broom, making piles of soot and debris—a button and the tops of cans, pieces of cardboard, gum wrappers and hardened bread crusts. Traces of fishy lox, coffee beans and apples, filled the closed-up air. The emptiness around him echoed with the stomp and bluster of the ice man, the clink of the two sweating bottles of milk that the milkman used to set on the doorstep before dawn, the tinkle of the door chime, and his father's warm 'Shalom' each time a customer walked in. Nate could see his mother bustling around the store in a spotless butcher's apron.

When he looked at the piles he'd swept up, he felt gloomy. Finally, feeling the weight of failure, he left them like dusty hillocks on the wooden floor.

Ever since his father died, Mamma hardly brushed her hair. She pinned it in a careless doorknob with pieces falling down around her neck. Six days a week, she bent over a treadle sewing machine in Levy's sweatshop, stitching lace-trimmed ruffles onto linen shirtwaists. Each day was seven shirtwaists long.

"Five bucks, rich ladies pay at Kaufmanns for those *shmates*," she'd told Nathan, wheezing and sipping cold tea in the tiny flat they'd shared with Golda and two boarders since they'd lost the store.

Sometimes, when Nate glanced her way, he thought she was her shadow. He felt the chill inside her and wondered if she too was getting ready to die.

***

Nate first saw the Irish girl at O'Malley's Pub, passing out mugs of dark, thick-foamed beer. In a crown of golden braids and cheeks that glowed through ivory skin like Golda's china doll, she was so beautiful and so remote, that all the men were staring.

A few days later, Nathan recognized her walking toward him on Linton Street. She was wearing a navy woolen shawl over a ruffled blouse like the ones his mother sewed. Walking proudly, eyes ahead, she pushed a leather baby carriage.

"G-good morning," he stammered.

She raised her honey-colored lashes, surveyed him, and lowered them again.

Maybe she remembers me, he felt breathless. Heat crept up behind his ears; his collar suddenly felt too tight. Turning quickly, he strode into the stogie factory, sat down on his four legged stool and opened up the *Yiddish Daily Forward*. His job was reading Yiddish newspapers to the four workers. So their minds would be occupied while their hands split tobacco leaves and rolled them into piles of fat brown stogies.

Hoping she'd come by again, Nathan moved his stool so he could see the street.

The door was open all year long. Otherwise the heat and smells of tobacco and unwashed feet grew unbearable.

Day and night his dreams were full of her. Finally, he walked over to O'Malley's Pub and asked Oly O'Malley about her.

"Is it sweet on 'er ye are?" Oly grinned and poked him in the ribs.

"Just curious."

She'd come from Ireland, O'Malley said. "Name's Brita, by the way. Her parents got the influenza ... died on shipboard and got buried in the sea before they ever saw America. Somehow she'd lost her shoes during the passage, and walked the icy streets in a pair of borrowed slippers till she fainted. A man found her and took her in. Without no Mamma to take care, ain't no wonder she

133

got 'erself in trouble," Oly shook his head. Nathan sighed. It was a sad story.

"Too bad me or the Missus didn't find her first." Oly shook his head. "She's a sweet one, too. Only just fifteen."

One gray morning several weeks later, Nate glanced up from the *Pittsburg Press*, and there she was walking by.

"Good day," he hailed her from his perch and waved.

She turned her head. Barely lifting her fingers from the buggy handle, she squinted into the dimness. On that day, the baby was sitting up and playing with her fingers. A few straw-colored wisps stuck out below the brim of her white bonnet.

Nate had overheard his mother gossiping about her with the other *yentas*. They'd called the girl a harlot and a Jezebel. With sharp voices and downturned mouths, they said she picked up money on the side, doing whatever men wanted in the back room of the saloon. "In my opinion," Aunt Golda maintained, "she should get a job in sewing or laundry like a respectable person, before one of those lowlifes gives her another baby."

"So who can wear starched blouses on five cents a week?" Sarah shot back.

"Brita," Nathan whispered, and her name was gentle on his tongue. Could someone so innocent-looking really be a harlot? The yentas were convinced of it. The girl walked by most mornings now. She greeted him and almost smiled.

Gentile, a non-Jew, he reminded himself sternly, *shiksa*. Traif, his best friend Mac would call her—forbidden flesh. Nate wondered what she did with the faceless men who paid her to do whatever they wanted. He imagined them with oil-slicked hair and gold watch chains across their vests. Mac bragged about the Shiksas he'd *shtupped* in a river shack some of the older boys rented to take bad girls to.

"*Shtuping*," Mac spoke expansively, hands in his pockets, "is like hot lava. Time you tried it, Nathan."

The bragging irritated Nate, who trusted his friend in almost everything. He suspected Mac was fibbing.

"Good day," he said to Brita the next day. The wind had blown away the soot and smog, and he'd just warned himself for the hundredth time not to get involved, because she was a *shiksa* with a baby.

She smiled back, "Good day to ye." Her hair was warm and golden in the sunlight. At the IKS dance the week before, Ellie Finkel had dragged Nathan out on the dance floor for all three ladies' choices. Wearing a black skirt and a blouse starched to cardboard, she'd pressed so close Nate had to lean way back. Her hands were sweaty and her gardenia perfume made Nathan want to sneeze. All the girls at those dances looked a little like his mother. He could see them parading into the future, praying *moitzes* and lighting candles, their hair pulled tighter, cheekbones sharper every year. Smelling of *kugel* and *gefllte fish*, they poured coffee from endless pots, all the while gossiping and *kvetching* about the sadness in their lives.

Because, God forbid, God's chosen people shouldn't always be thinking about the suffering God chose them for, he thought bitterly.

After a few weeks Nate would light a stogie when he saw her and stroll casually along beside her for a ways—past shopkeepers setting up their merchandise on the sidewalk, past *shysters* and peddlers with fat packs, past churches, and synagogues.

The baby's name was Carolyn. She greeted Nate with smiles and gurgles. Brita had a way of talking that sounded like a song. She told him how she'd crossed the cold November sea—sick and squeamish the whole way, how her mother and father had sickened with a terrible flu and died in an epidemic that buried half the steerage passengers at sea. One day, when icy swells were seeping through the floorboards, Brita leapt for the metal ladder by her bunk and lost both shoes in the surging water. She never found them. The ladder made a nasty gash. In fact, she still had the scar.

"Right here." Stooping, she raised her skirt and rubbed a finger over a raised red scar on the inside of her knee. Nate could see a crescent underneath her black wool stocking.

He told her about Alfie's accident, and how his Pappa died so unexpected, when things were just beginning to feel right. He told her how much he loved books, and shared his dreams of writing some day for the Pittsburgh Press. And now, there was too little time and not enough money. In fact he confessed, he was afraid he might be reading Yiddish papers in the stogie factory for the rest of his life.

One morning, the baby wouldn't settle down, Brita tried sticking a finger in her mouth. She spit the finger right back out, stiffened her little body, and started to wail.

"What is it Caro? What's the matter?" Brita lifted her out of the buggy. She hummed and patted, while Nathan pushed the empty carriage. Finally, the baby screwed her face up and cried till she turned purple.

Nate decided he would wait a few more years to be a father.

"Could be she's hungry." Brita frowned. "Maybe I should feed her."

"Can I come?" Nate was surprised at himself.

She led him down a narrow flight cut into the earth. When his eyes adjusted, he made out a white splash of tablecloth, a wooden rocker beside a small iron stove, a teakettle.

Brita settled in the rocker, laid a flannelette blanket on her shoulder and began to fumble underneath. "Nathan, will ye' please to turn around?"

He sat nearby on her cot, fingering the stitches in her patchwork quilt. Once, by accident, he turned and caught a glimpse of full flesh, sloping toward a dark-tipped nipple. He gaped, startled by her softness. He'd never seen a breast before. The breath caught in his throat, and he forced himself to concentrate on a row of teacups hanging from a shelf. Studying their patterns, Nate wished he could ask Mac how a person got from looking to that thing Mac said was like hot lava. When he tried to picture it, he was afraid it might be violent.

Moments later, he snuck another glance. Brita held the baby in the crook of her arm and pushed the rocker with her toe. Carolyn sucked noisily, filling up mouth and belly, kneading at the blanket with a tiny fist. Nate could almost see the milk gathering in rivulets and squirting in the baby's mouth. Doubtless it was warm, like Brita. He wondered how it tasted.

Now, Brita sat the baby up and thumped her back. A loud burp sent a bluish stream of milk dribbling back out over her lip.

"That milk looks a little pale," Nate blurted, before he could stop himself. "Is it all right?"

"Nate, you Goose." She reached over and patted his arm. "That's the way it comes." She raised the baby to her shoulder and fumbled with the buttons on her shirtwaist.

"Now fer all yer waiting can I fix ye a cuppa tea?" she asked in that strange and lilting way she had.

"Please," Nathan whispered and grasped the corner of the blanket.

Before she had a chance to say yes or no, he'd folded it back. Breathing the milky whiteness from her skin, he felt soft inside and hard down there. He laid his fingers gently on the flesh that swelled with every breath she took. For a moment, she was still. Nate's heart was pounding in his ears. Did he dare to slide the hand a wee bit further?

"No more," she grabbed his wrist and set his hand in his own lap. Sighing, she rose and laid the baby on the quilt.

Nathan felt like crying.

Then she was back in the rocker with her buttons fastened, reaching out to take his hands. "Have you heard the things they say about me?" Her eyes were deep and troubled.

He nodded.

"They are lying. I-I've never been a p-prostitute."

"So then what?" Nate asked softly.

"The man who rescued me...h-he forced me." She was sobbing. "Never another time till I marry." She crossed herself.

"Then I will marry you," Nathan said simply.

"Hush." Her finger touched his lips. "Nathan, yer my best and only friend. She smelled of starch and milk as sweet as the vanilla ice cream he'd licked from a spoon after he and Mamma locked the store, so tired and spent that only ice cream seemed to soothe them.

In the days that followed, Nate didn't go back to Brita's room. Instead, he pushed the baby carriage, sometimes talking, sometimes silent. When their fingers touched by accident, or the sun shone on Brita's upturned face, Nate felt like dancing right there in the street. For the rest of his life, he would wonder which of his mother's friends had seen him with the Irish girl. And spread it to the other yentas, who'd picked up tidbits and tore at them like crows. Especially the tasty rumor that Nathan Aaron Lindenberg had been seen leaving the room of the *shiksa* with the bastard child who worked for Oly O'Malley at the tavern.

***

Three of Sarah's friends had come to her, and Ida Wise even had the *chutzpah* to suggest the girl could be expecting another baby from Sarah's Nathan. What galled her most was that someone had seen Nathan leaving the girls flat in daylight. "At least if he was going to a whore, he could sneak out in the dark like a respectable person!" She ranted to her sister, Golda.

"Boys grow up," Golda shrugged. "So, *nu*? Who can prevent it? Your Nathan is becoming a man."

"On top of that, a *shiksa*," Sarah fumed, pacing the tiny front room each night when sleep evaded her. And she herself, the daughter of a *shohet*! Even if Pappa were the laughing-stock, he was still a *Cohen*—Right? She imagined a widening spiral of catastrophes. God forbid, her Nathan should be lunatic enough to marry in a Catholic church. He might as well be dead. She'd have to sit *shiva*h for him. Jewish law demanded it. Sarah began coughing and gripped the back of a kitchen chair until the spell passed. Wiping her lips on the back of her hand, she sunk down at the table. She'd coughed for months now, her hacking like an echo of the choking gasps that shook her Mamma till she weakened and died.

"Mamma," she whispered. When Sarah was only six, she'd watched her mother die of consumption, like drowning in her narrow bed. They'd left her in Riga, under a gray stone on a grassy moll in the Jewish cemetery. Now she was glad her Mamma hadn't lived to see the disappointment of America—the grinding work and fading hopes until there was nothing left except children who no longer did their duty by their parents. God she was worn out, thirty-nine years old and ancient. She'd never thought she'd get as sour as Golda. But, Nathan with a Catholic strumpet! Who could bear it? She threw up her hands. She'd worked all his life so she could send him to Medical School. She'd expected to live out her old age with him in an apartment full of sunshine, with a room for her that had a brocade chaise lounge. She'd never questioned he'd be married in a synagogue, to a Jewish girl who knew what it was to respect a mother-in-law, and make a beautiful *challah*, and put a savory *cholent* in the oven, with a nice beef bone, prunes and onions, to eat on Saturday. One tear meandered down her cheek and she licked it from the corner of her mouth. It tasted salty.

***

"He's right on Center Avenue with the harlot and her child!" Ida Wise, that busybody, was pounding on the door.

"All right, all right, don't have a heart attack already."

Sarah hurried to undo the latch. Her friend stood panting in the hall, her black shawl falling off one shoulder. The peacock feather on her hat *farblondzshet*.

142

Sarah grabbed her own shawl from the coat tree and headed out behind her. "Shush!" Ida grabbed her elbow and shoved her along the tenement wall. Sarah craned her neck around the corner, and there was Nathan with the strumpet! Pushing a buggy yet! The whore was hanging from his elbow, like a swooning ninny.

Sarah groaned. Then, unable to stand another minute, she hobbled around the corner.

"*Kein Ayin Hara* Nathan Lindenberg!" she shouted. "The *Evil Eye* has got you now."

Nate looked up in time to see quick approach, her waving hands and yelling mouth, "Jezebel" Her hand darted through the air, and cracked on Brita's cheek.

The girl fingered the rising crimson palm print.

"Mamma," Nate gasped. "Are you demented?"

Carolyn woke up screaming, and Brita bent to soothe her.

"A *shanda*, Son! That woman is a no-good hussy." She grabbed Nathan's shoulders and began shaking him.

Two blocks down, the hoods in front of *Cheezy's* heard the uproar. They stomped on their cigarettes, jammed their hands in their pockets and swaggered toward the fracas. The neighborhood spilled out of tenements and pushcarts, while the yentas made a semi-circle at the front, leaning forward in their black dresses like fascinated birds. Sarah struck at Brita's face and kicked her in the shins.

143

"Stop!" The girl reached out and grasped Sarah's upper arms. "Stop. Please. Do you understand?" When Brita's hands dropped, Sarah stumbled backward and landed in a heap of black skirts. Momentarily, she was quiet.

Then she ripped her dress straight down the front to the waist, till her chemise showed, and her gray old skin. *"Yitkadal, v'ytkadash sh'mei raba."*

She chanted, *davening*, and yanking at her hair.

The crowd squeezed closer. Nathan dropped his head in shame. These were people he had known all his life. He'd seen them laughing and talking, even crying. Now they were spectators at his disgrace. His mind was seething with ideas and yet, he was paralyzed. How he wished his mother hadn't come with her drabness and her flock of vicious *yentas*, to tear at him, and at the girl who had no mother of her own to take up for her.

"Out of the way." Oly O'Malley pushed aside the row of old women. "What're ye doin' girlie, brawling with a crazy woman?" There was laughter. Oly circled Brita's shoulders with his arm. "Let's get ye home and clean ye up a bit."

"Nathan?" Brita's eyes were flashed blue ice; her braids had tumbled to her waist.

To him, she'd never looked so beautiful. His mother's eyes were brown.

144

"B-brita, I-I can't," he stammered. "Please understand. A mother is a mother. Do you see?"

"No. I do not."

A vice was closing in on Nathan's ribs. His mother spread her fingers on the dirt and raised herself on trembling arms. Knees knocking against her skirt, she stood. Then, with the lightness of an organ grinder's monkey, she sprung and raked her nails down Brita's cheek.

"Ye'll stop it now!" barked O'Malley and put his bulk between them. Carolyn started crying and Brita reached for her. The scratches filled with crimson drops that trickled down her cheek and spattered on the baby's hair. Nate looked at Brita, proud as ever, and ached so much inside that he could barely breathe.

Righteous and bent, his mamma stood. "Son," she ordered, "Take me home." Then, gathering her rags around her like queen's robes, she spat twice on the ground, wound her arm through Nathan's and steered him toward Cliff Street.

After a few minutes, Nate jerked his arm away. Turning, he retraced his steps. The buggy stood abandoned in the melting crowd. Grabbing the handle, he ran behind its bouncing wheels down Cliff Street, calling out to Oly O'Malley and the Irish girl to wait for him.

Epilogue

Dad has had a heart attack. I fly to Honolulu, incongruous among holiday bound tourists. In a room that smells of antiseptic, my father's body is a small mound under a cotton blanket, a sandwich tucked neatly into a wrinkle-free rectangle. One arm rests on top. A thumbprint of small blue veins smudges the inside of his elbow. His fingers curl, relaxed as those of a sleeping child. Plastic tubes, taped to the back of his hand, drip liquid into him from a bottle on a shiny pole. Computer screens register my father's inner workings in green graphics and shrill beeps.

His head on the pillow is small, his skin sallow and jaw shrunken. Slightly bruised lips protrude around a breathing tube. His chest rises and falls to the suck and blow of a respirator. Only his hair, white and wavy, curiously uncrushable, seems untouched by the ordeal. I smooth it with my palm and stroke the parchment forehead. Lifting his hand, I curl my fingers underneath. For a moment I am little again, my hand held safely inside my Dad's.

He has been on this respirator for 18 hours, until my brother, Marc and I can fly to Honolulu from the Mainland. His future is precarious. When the machine stops breathing for him, he may die.

The nurse slides a light green drape along an oval rod above his bed. It makes a shower curtain sound. Mother, Marc, and I stand with arms around each other's backs, breathing in one breath.

The tube sticks then slides neatly out of my fathers' mouth. His lips sag against his teeth. His skin grows even paler. Reddish blonde lashes flicker up. Reveal opaque unmoving eyes. I wish I had two silver dollars to close them.

All at once, my father's lips move. His mouth opens.

"Goddamn," he croaks, "I'm glad they finally took that thing out of my mouth."

He sleeps awhile. And we unwind. Perhaps the odds are in our favor. The nurse brings coffee and buttery wheat toast from the kitchenette. The coffee tastes of paper cup.

***

The funeral we had come for was postponed. Our time together was a weeklong gift, the hospital room a sanctuary.

"Y'know, Sue," Dad was reflective, "I used to wake up in the night and worry about work. I haven't worked for years and I still wake up. Maybe I worry about dying."

"About death Dad, more likely." My voice lowered to a whisper. My question was against the unspoken rules. "You were only three when your father died. Please Dad. Tell me about it…"

I waited eyes down. "Dad?" When I looked up, he'd fallen asleep.

The following Tuesday, my father's breathing slowed so gradually we hardly noticed; until his lips turned gray. Mother, her face like melting paraffin, perched on his bed and held his hand. Her feet dangled in the air. They'd been married almost forty nine years.

My eyes moved to the green curtain. No longer green but filmy white; it shimmered as if thinning in the antiseptic air. Through it I could make out a window and a dark gigantic sky.

My wrist moved the gauzy curtain and my feet spanned the distance to the window. Below me, as far as I could see, was a vast starry ocean. Through a hole in the glittering, more distant than an airplane view, I could make out ragged outlines—mountains, land, and a ribbon of water.

I took a sharp breath and hold it, terrified and somehow blessed to be looking through the ceiling on the world beneath our world.

***

The memorial service takes place beside the swimming pool at the Mott Smith Laniloa condominiums, Honolulu. We sit in a circle of gray folding chairs—Mother, my brother, Marc, my husband, and our three children. Marc's best friend Paul, our brother by ties and loving, has offered to lead the *Kaddish*.

My brother reads the eulogy, scribbled in pencil on a blue lined scrap of yellow legal paper.

"Mommy, why are you crying," asks my son, Robbie, catching my tears on his fingers and licking them. What shall I say to him about my father? To my son, my father is a grandfather.

A grandfather is an old man with a patch over one eye and a cigar butt in the corner of his mouth who has trouble waiting for dinner time. A grandfather is someone who pats him on the head and asks how nursery school is going.

Robbie climbs up in my lap. His child's arms wrap around my neck. What shall I tell him? My son never saw my father hold an audience in the palm of his hand, or watched him walk through a torn and burning city ghetto, greeting people, shaking hands…

His voice goes on but my mind is no longer with my son … I am eight years old, dressed in yellow jammies. My father sits reading the paper on brown and beige upholstered armchair. His stocking feet are on the matching ottoman.

I shinny up over his bony knees and twine my arms around his neck. "Daddy, stop reading. I have a very important question."

"What is it Kid?" He folds the paper and lays it on the floor beside his chair.

"Daddy," I ask my mouth nested, tucked behind his neck. What will happen when I die?"

He thinks a minute. "I don't know, Kid," he replies finally, one corner of his mustache twitching. "You don't have to worry though because when you're dead, you won't be there to worry about it."

Paul is leading *Kaddish* from the *Union Prayer Book*. He wears khaki pants, a light blue button down shirt and a black *yarmulke*. He is not *davening*. But he is chanting and his voice is deep and beautiful.

I close my eyes. The cadence of the Hebrew words stirs thousand-year-old memories. I open them and glance across the turquoise pool with its blue rope and blue and white floaters. A breeze disturbs the surface and it breaks up in a mottled sheen. I catch a whiff of chlorine and my eyes water.

I shake my head, trying to fathom what I see.

Reflected in the water, I can make out our circle of chairs. But we are not sitting on them. From the corners of the pool, men drift in on silent feet and stand in front of the chairs.

Yarmulke covered heads, blonde, bald, dark and curly. *Tallit* fringes floating in the golden light like sea anemones. The men are swaying back and forth, deep voices chanting in rhythmic cadence with Paul and with me. *"Yitkadal, v'ytkadash sh'mei raba."*

Glossary

Bar Mitzvah for a boy, *B'nai Mitzvah* (gender neutral), or
Bat Mitzvah for a girl ~ celebration at age 13 of coming of
    age and when the young person   first reads from
    the Torah

Boychik ~ young man

Challah ~ braided egg bread made for Sabbath

Charoset or *Haroset* ~ a mixture of chopped nuts and
    apples, wine, and spices that is eaten at the
    Seder meal on Passover

Chassid or *Hasidic* ~ a Godly man

Cheder ~ Jewish religious school

Cholent ~ stew

Chutzpa ~ gall or nerve

Cohen ~ priest (Jewish)

Daven ~ rocking while praying, standing up

Dumkoph ~ dumb or an idiot

Dybbuks ~ wandering spirit or ghost

Feh ~ ick, like a bad taste

Fegeleh ~ also slang for gay

Farblondzshet~ bewildered, confused

Gay Avek ~ go away

Gefllte fish ~ a fish dish traditionally eaten at Passover

Goniff ~ a thief

Gotenu ~ oh my God

Goyim ~ non-Jews

Hagaddah ~ Passover prayer book

Kaddish ~ a prayer said in remembrance of the dead

Kein Ayin Hara ~ said to ward off evil eye when one has celebrated beauty too much

Kasshruth ~ obedience to the kosher laws or ways to preparing food

Kike ~ an ethnic slur against Jews

Kippa or Yamulke ~ skull cap

Kugel ~ a potato or pasta casserole

Kvell ~ brag about, celebrate

Kvetch ~ complain (the K is pronounced)

Manischewitz ~ a kind of sweet wine

Matzos ~ flat bread or crackers eaten at Passover

Mazeltov ~ congratulations, good job

Mench ~ a good person

Mitzvah ~ blessing

Motzies ~ blessings chanted over wine, candles and bread

Nebbish ~ a blah person

Nu ~ what or like shrugging your shoulder

Pesach ~ Passover

Reb ~ Rabbi

Schvitzbath ~ Sweat bath

Seder ~ Passover meal with prayers and specific foods

Shah ~ expression of disdain

Shalom ~ good day or peace be with you

Shanda ~ shame

Shiksa ~ impure, used to refer or a non-Jewish woman

Shiva ~ a one week period of mourning after the death
    of a family member

Shlock ~ crap, bull shit

Shmaltz ~ chicken fat or slang for 'oily' communication

Shmate ~ rag, often refers to a piece of clothing

Shohet ~ Kosher butcher

Shtupp ~ slang for sex

Shyster ~ an unscrupulous person

Tallit (*Tallis*) ~ prayer shawl

Torah ~ first five books of the Hebrew Bible (*Genesis,
    Exodus, Leviticus, Numbers and Deuteronomy*)

Traif ~ food that is not kosher

Yarmulke or Kippa ~ skull cap

Yenta ~ gossipy old lady

Zayde ~ grandfather